# CLOSE-UP

## Forensic Photography

THE CRIME SCENE CLUB: 5 FACT AND FICTION

# THE CRIME SCENE CLUB: FACT AND FICTION

# CLOSE-UP

## Forensic Photography

Kenneth McIntosh

Mason Crest Publishers

# Close-Up: Forensic Photography

MASON CREST PUBLISHERS INC.
370 Reed Road
Broomall, Pennsylvania 19008
(866)MCP-BOOK (toll free)
www.masoncrest.com

First Printing

9 8 7 6 5 4 3 2 1

ISBN 978-1-4222-0259-3 (series)
                    Library of Congress Cataloging-in-Publication Data

McIntosh, Kenneth, 1959–
  Close-up : forensic photography / by Kenneth McIntosh.
      p. cm. — (Crime Scene Club ; case #5)
  Summary: When the members of the Crime Scene Club visit Los Angeles, they become involved in an investigation into what appears to be the accidental death of a surfer.
  Includes bibliographical references and index.
  ISBN 978-1-4222-0251-7      ISBN 978-1-4222-1454-1
  [1. Surfing—Fiction. 2. Murder—Fiction. 3. Clubs—Fiction. 4. Pho-tography—Fiction. 5. California, Southern—Fiction. 6. Mystery and detective stories.] I. Title.
  PZ7.M1858Cl 2009
  [Fic]—dc22
                              2008023308

Design by MK Bassett-Harvey.
Produced by Harding House Publishing Service, Inc.
www.hardinghousepages.com
Cover design by MK Bassett-Harvey.
Cover and interior illustrations by Casey Sanborn.
Printed in Malaysia.

# CONTENTS

# INTRODUCTION

The sound of breaking glass. A scream. A shot. Then . . . silence. Blood, fingerprints, a bullet, a skull, fire debris, a hair, shoeprints—enter the wonderful world of forensic science. A world of searching to find clues, collecting that which others cannot see, testing to find answers to seemingly impossible questions, and testifying to juries so that justice will be served. A world where curiosity, love of a puzzle, and gathering information are basic. The books in this series will take you to this world.

## The CSI Effect

The TV show *CSI: Crime Scene Investigator* became so widely popular that *CSI: Miami* and *CSI: NY* followed. This forensic interest spilled over into *Bones* (anthropology); *Crossing Jordan* and *Dr. G* (medical examiners); *New Detectives* and *Forensic Files*, which cover all the forensic disciplines. Almost every modern detective story now involves forensic science. Many fiction books are written, some by forensic scientists such as Kathy Reichs (anthropology) and Ken Goddard (criminalistics and crime scene), as well as textbooks such as *Criminalistics* by Richard Saferstein. Other crime fiction authors are Sir Arthur Conan Doyle (Sherlock Holmes), Thomas Harris (*Red Dragon*), Agatha Christie (Hercule Poirot) and Ellis Peters, whose hero is a monk, Cadfael, an ex-Crusader who solves crimes. The list goes on and on—and I encourage you to read them all!

The spotlight on forensic science has had good *and* bad effects, however. Because the books and TV shows are so enjoyable, the limits of science have been blurred to make the plots more interesting. Often when students are intrigued by the TV shows and want to learn more, they have a rude awakening. The crime scene investigators on TV do the work of many professionals, including police officers, medical examiners, forensic laboratory scientists, anthropologists, and entomologists, to mention just a few. And all this in addition to processing crime scenes! Fictional instruments give test results at warp speed, and crimes are solved in forty-two minutes. Because of the overwhelming popularity of these shows, juries now expect forensic evidence in every case.

The books in this series will take you to both old and new forensic sciences, perhaps tweaking your interest in a career. If so, take courses in chemistry, biology, math, English, public speaking, and drama. Get a summer job in a forensic laboratory, courthouse, law enforcement agency, or an archeological dig. Seek internships and summer jobs (even unpaid). Skills in microscopy, instrumentation, and logical thinking will help you. Curiosity is a definite plus. You must read and understand procedures; take good notes; calculate answers; and prepare solutions. Public speaking and/or drama courses will make you a better speaker and a better expert witness. The ability to write clear, understandable reports aimed at nonscientists is a must. Salaries vary across the country and from agency to agency. You will never get rich, but you will have a satisfying, interesting career.

So come with me into this wonderful world called forensic science. You will be intrigued and entertained. These books are awesome!

—*Carla M. Noziglia MS, FAAFS*

# Prologue
# FLOATER

*Splash.*

The body hit the water, submerged briefly, then rested on the surface, bobbing gently on the waves, face downward. The next second, a red surfboard followed the corpse into the ocean, tethered to the body's right foot.

Voices from the nearby boat drifted over the inky water.

"You sure this is a good idea?"

"It's perfect."

"But they'll examine the body—"

"And say 'It's an accident. He died surfing, what a way to go.'"

"But that bruise where you nailed him—"

"Looks like the board hit his head. How sad."

"What if they search the house?"

"Won't happen, but if it does, I'll handle it. We wore gloves. Everything's spotless. Chill."

"Okay, but . . . this doesn't feel right."

"It's not every day you get away with murder. So don't worry, be happy." The voice chuckled. "Now start up the motor, but pull away slowly—make sure he doesn't float into the propeller. And keep the lights off until we're further out to sea."

The roar of the boat's engine shattered the silence, and the watercraft pulled away from the dead man, whose body rolled up and down in the vessel's wake. As the water calmed, the victim drifted with the waves, moving closer to shore with each swell. Just as the sun poked its bright orange face over the eastern hills, turning the ocean the fruity colors of tangerines and peaches, the stiffening body washed onto the sands of Neptune Cove.

# Chapter 1
# LIFE'S A BEACH

"Hey! I can't see the screen!" Wire struggled to contain his anger. Maeve was supposed to hold his PDA so he could follow the navigation program while driving. But instead, she carried on an animated discussion with Jessa, who sat behind them.

"I can't believe I've known you all this time and never seen your tattoos," Jessa exclaimed.

Wire glanced at Maeve, seated next to him, and noticed for the first time that her back, underneath the straps of her bikini top, was covered with a flock of tattooed bats, ascending from her waist and spreading out over her shoulders.

"How did you ever get permission to do that?" Jessa asked.

"Not hard. After Mom's had a few drinks, she'll sign anything I tell her to," Maeve replied.

"You should go to court and get emancipated," Wire commented. "That's what I did. But right now—will you please hold that PDA where I can see it."

"Oops." Maeve thrust the small electronic device in front of Wire's face.

"No! You're blocking my vision. Off to the side a little—okay, there, that's better." He glanced at the little red dot indicating their vehicle's GPS location, and the lines that represented roads. "Oh, crap."

"What?"

"Missed our intersection. Gotta turn around." He pulled the rented mini-van off the road, waited for a truck to zoom past, then headed back in the direction they had come. "Now will you please focus and keep that thing in place?"

*Mental note: never, ever, under any circumstance, go on another weeklong trip with three females.* As far as Wire was concerned, this LA vacation had started all wrong in the first place. Crime Scene Club, the unique partnership between the Flagstaff police department and Flagstaff Charter, was under strict orders not to involve its teen members with actual criminal cases; they had been involved with too many dangerous situations. Yet CSC had all kinds of money, thanks to its wealthy patron, so the authorities decided to throw this little "field trip" at the kids for a consolation prize. Apparently, the adults' thinking had gone like this: the club might not be able to use its forensic skills to solve actual crimes, but at least they could have fun. Then two members hadn't been able to make the trip—and that left Wire as the only male on the excursion, tagging along with Maeve the Goth chick, Jessa the wannabe hippie, and Detective Kwan, their chaperone.

Wire had almost backed out as well, and he would have—except for an instant message he'd received:

Can't wait to see you in person. I'm a little scared, but so excited.

We're perfect for each other in
cyber space—can you imagine what it
will be like to meet face-to-face?
Your girl, QT.

Wire knew QTAnimeChick only by her words sent over the Internet; he didn't even know her real name, but he did have one picture she had sent. He'd printed that picture in high-resolution format and taped it on the wall over his desktop monitor.

Wire lived alone in a trailer filled with electronics; he wouldn't change his home for anything, but sometimes it did get lonely. When that happened, he would look at QT's smiling face and dream. So—he had come on this trip so he could finally meet her. But so far, they had failed to get together. In fact, she wasn't replying to his phone calls or e-mails. And in the meantime. . . .

The club worked as a democracy, which was a really stupid idea, considering the female-male ratio was stacked three to one. The first day, Wire wanted to visit the Beverly Hills Spy Store, so he could check out the high-tech gadgets. Then the girls decided to go to the so-called happiest place on earth, where tourists mindlessly gather like lemmings and pay a ton of money for a day's admission: Disneyland Park. Wire wound up floating past caves full of phony pirates, watching rubber animals off the prow of the jungle cruise boat, and wishing he could tear the heads off those crazy-making mechanical parrots in the singing Polynesian hut thing.

Then yesterday, he suggested they all go to the big comic convention. Artists from Marvel, Dark Horse, real creative geniuses, and some amazingly talented game-makers would all be there. But did the girls want to go to ComicCon? No. So Wire spent the day tagging along behind them, hot and frustrated, as they wasted their time going in and out of clothing stores on Rodeo Drive.

And this morning, the tour from Hades took a downturn, if that was possible. Wire had begged for a day at the technology show in the Downtown Convention Center. Sony, Macintosh, Toshiba— all the big manufacturers were in town with their newest dream machines. He tried logic: "Isn't it my turn to pick our itinerary? This would actually have some bearing on forensic science, and isn't that the reason why we're here?"

Nope. Lupe Arellano—who hadn't even come on the trip—had set up surfing lessons for the three of them with her cousin's boyfriend and some old guy. Wire could barely swim; no way he was going to drown himself for an inane macho sport. Yet, here they were, headed for some forsaken spot in the boonies called Neptune Cove.

Adding insult to injury, he was stuck playing taxi-driver for the girls. Detective Kwan had eaten something bad at the seafood restaurant last night, and this morning, she was too sick to get out of bed. Maeve was nervous about driving after her recent accident, and Jessa was such a tree-hugger that she rarely drove anything beside her bicycle. So: "Wire, you've gotta drive us to the beach."

He often felt unappreciated in life, but this trip was the worst. Not an intelligent stop on the tour, no word from the girl of his dreams, and now he was playing chaperone for Vampirella and Patchouli Girl. Oh, and: "Wire, you can take pictures," Ms. Kwan had said as she handed him the big black case with the CSC photography equipment. Why couldn't Jessa at least do that?

He looked again at the flashing light and little lines on his PDA; at least Maeve was holding it where he could see it now. According to the navigation system, they were almost at their destination.

"Ooh, I think I see them," Jessa cried gleefully. Ahead, on the side of the road, Wire spotted two men: a gray-haired, bare-chested guy, and a thuggish looking teen in a hooded sweatshirt and shorts. The two of them were seated on the rear bumper of a rusty surf-van. "This is gonna be so awesome," Jessa squealed, literally bouncing up and down with excitement.

*Yeah, right. I just wish QT would send me an IM. Something good has gotta come out of this vacation from hell.*

# Chapter 2
# THE DISAPPEARING CRIME SCENE

"Four-foot swells," Grizz Sanchez noted with satisfaction. "They're coming in sets of three, curling from south to north. Perfect," Grizz felt the cool sea breeze tickle the hairs on his chest and the sunshine warming his shoulders. On the other side of the hill, seagulls cawed.

"Remind me why we're wasting a perfectly nice day babysitting barnies?"

Grizz glanced down at the young man sitting on the rear bumper of the van beside him. Dirk's green eyes glared from under the hood of his sweater, but Grizz was used to the teen's sour disposition; he could overlook Dirk's idiosyncrasies and appreciate his finer qualities. Grizz had literally taken Dirk off the street, gotten him out of trouble with the law, and taught him how to run a surf shop and find his way in society. "As I recall, your girl Keisha set this thing up," Grizz told him.

"Yeah, her cousin Lupe was coming with something called Crime Scene Club from Arizona. But Keisha is in a competition up in Santa Cruz, and her cousin Lupe isn't on this trip—so how come we have to hold these dorks' hands and keep them from drowning?"

Grizz pulled a clove cigarette from the back hatch of the Vanagon, lit it, and took a puff. "If you do a favor for someone, just out of the kindness of your heart, the universe will reward ya."

"Bull. Gimme a cig."

"Nope. You might make it to the pro circuit this year. They don't look kindly on young athletes smoking."

Dirk made a face. "So says the legendary soul surfer who's been smoking for how long?"

Grizz shook his head. "Too long. Wish I could quit. Really."

The van's stereo was turned on, and a radio newscaster's voice spoke from the speakers in the rear of the vehicle: "Former film star Lance Grant announced his bid for Congress today."

Dirk spat on the road. "What a poser. He was in those *Beach Umbrella* movies, acting like the Great Kahuna. I swear he never even got his hair wet."

"Hope he makes a better politician than an actor," Grizz agreed.

Just then, they both noticed a mini-van slowing down and pulling off the road behind their vehicle.

"Guess this is them," Grizz said cheerfully.

"Freakin' barnies," Dirk muttered.

The doors of the mini-van opened; three teens stepped out and headed toward them. One, a tall, thin young man with long straight hair and John Lennon eyeglasses, put out a hand. "Hi, I'm Wire."

"Grizz Sanchez, owner of Grizzly Surfboard Shop. Pleased to meet you." *This guy is gonna drown, I know it*, Grizz thought, noting the boy's nerdy appearance and sorry physique. *But there's something special going on with this kid. I sense good karma here.*

A blond girl with long matted locks, dressed in a one-piece Hawaiian-pattern bathing suit, ran up to them. "Hi, I'm Jessa. This is so exciting."

Grizz noted Jessa's tightly muscled legs and tanned limbs. *Might make a surfer out of this one.*

"Hi, I'm Dirk." The young man jumped in front of Grizz, grabbed Jessa's hand, and pumped it.

*Think, boy, think.* Grizz tried to send a mental message to the headstrong young man, recalling a conversation they'd had just the day before.

"You mean I can only have one girl at a time?" Dirk had been incredulous.

Grizz had nodded. "Yes, if you're going steady it is just one girl—*uno, no mas. Comprende?*"

Dirk had stared at him, gape-jawed, and Grizz had sighed with exasperation. "How can you be so dense, boy? You're lucky to have a classy young woman like Keisha. So treat her like a jewel, let her develop the relationship her own way—don't push yourself on her. And yes, if you want to be her boyfriend, she is your *one* girl now."

"Whoa." Dirk had appeared shocked.

Now, as they stood on the roadside meeting these kids, Grizz hoped that Dirk would recall that discussion.

"Hi, I'm Maeve." A teenage girl with a mop of black hair, black makeup, and a black bikini stepped up and put out her hand. "I've gotta warn ya, I've probably done something in my lifetime to make the ocean gods pretty angry, so—who knows what might happen out there."

*And I thought we had all the nuts out here in California.*

Dirk turned his attention to Wire. "You going surfing? Where's your swimsuit?"

"I'm not going in the ocean. I'm here to take pictures," the bespectacled teen replied.

"Good idea. You don't look too fit." Dirk smirked.

*Easy, boy, easy. Let's work on making some positive energy here.*

Jessa intervened in the discussion. "So, can we get started? I've wanted to surf for—practically my whole life." She was wide-eyed and beaming.

"You bet!" Dirk replied. "I'll be your private coach. Grizz, you can teach . . . Spooky here." He nodded toward Maeve.

She made a face at him.

Grizz tried to ignore the unpleasantness. "We have foam boards in the back of the bus. They're the best way to learn. If everyone will grab a board, we'll head down to the beach."

Jessa squealed and jumped to grab a board. Maeve and Dirk did the same.

Wire sighed. "I'll get the camera gear from our rental car."

*Poor kid sounds miffed. Don't blame him,* Grizz thought. *He seems like a fish outta water here.*

The five walked around the hillock and started down a steep path leading to the concealed cove that Grizz had chosen for its privacy. B*etter to learn surfing without having to fight off a crowd in the*

*water.* At the head of the line, Jessa turned a corner, then let out a yell.

"There's a man lying on the beach. Looks like he's injured!" Her voice caught, came out in a squeak. "Or dead!"

*What the heck?* Wire was trailing the group, lugging the big padded case that held CSC's photographic equipment. He saw Grizz run ahead and kneel beside a figure that lay at the edge of the water. It was a man, in his thirties Wire guessed, wearing a short-sleeved wetsuit. A sharp-nosed red surfboard lay on the sand next to him.

Wire watched as the old guy felt for the man's pulse; Grizz was apparently used to giving first aid, but now he shook his head. "Cold and stiff. Nothing to do but call the police."

Dirk and Maeve stared at the body, apparently fascinated. Jessa put her hand to her mouth and walked away. Grizz looked down at the corpse, a sad look on his face.

"Who is he?" Maeve was peering at the dead guy's face.

"Some dude," Dirk answered.

"He sure looks familiar." She squatted down next to the body.

"Yeah," Grizz agreed. "I feel like I've seen him somewhere. Just can't recall where."

Wire spoke into his Bluetooth, listened, then said to the others, "Neptune PD says all their officers are on assignment, but they'll have a detective here in forty minutes to an hour."

Dirk snorted. "Lotta good that'll do."

"What do you mean?" Maeve asked.

Grizz answered for him. "I assume they want a detective to look over the scene—but there won't be any 'scene' to investigate by the time he gets here."

Wire's eyebrows went up. "Believe me, we know enough not to mess with a suspected crime scene."

"Not you. The tide," Dirk explained. "It's coming in—and this guy's half-covered with water already. An hour from now, he'll be drifting."

"Well…" Wire was quickly adjusting his thoughts. "I suppose it doesn't matter that much anyway. I mean, he obviously drowned. It's not like this is the actual scene where he died."

Grizz gave him a skeptical look, but Wire wasn't worried. The old dude might know more than he did about waves, but Wire knew his crimes scenes. "He washed in from the ocean," he continued. "And the only tracks near the body are ours." He pointed to their bare footprints in the sand. "He's dressed for surfing, and he's tied to his board. Looks pretty clear."

"And this?" The older man pointed to a deep gash on the dead man's right temple.

"Hit by a skeg?" Dirk wondered.

Grizz shook his head. "I've seen lots of people get hit by their fins—some real bad—never saw one looked like this. Nope, there's something unnatural about this poor soul's death."

"Are you sure?" Wire demanded.

Grizz shot him a look. *Okay, so maybe the guy knows more than I do about this.* Wire mopped his brow. "All right, we have a situation that our expert thinks is suspicious—and law enforcement won't be here until the scene is literally washed out. So. . ."

"Time to ask, 'WWKD?'" Maeve suggested.

"Huh?" Dirk looked at her like she was crazy.

"'What would Kwan do?'" the girl explained.

"She's the detective who works with our club," Wire added. "She's back at our hotel, sick now." He paused for a moment, then snapped into focus. "We need to preserve this scene until it's documented. We've already contaminated the site with our presence. Mr. Sanchez, if you would, sir, could you back away from the body, retracing your footsteps? Everyone else, do the same and then stay away from the corpse."

Dirk rolled his eyes, but Grizz nodded and did as the younger man requested.

"Can I help?" Maeve asked Wire.

"I'm going to take pictures of everything—our only way to document this site before the tide comes in. I'll connect the camera to my PDA, and you can type in notes to accompany the shots. Unless you can think of a better way to go at this?"

"Sounds good." She shivered in her swimsuit.

"Where's Jessa?"

"She's feeling sick."

"Don't blame her—she's seen too many dead bodies lately, I guess. Dirk, Mr. Sanchez—would you two look in the sand, starting about five feet out from the body, for anything that might be connected to this guy's death?"

"Things like?" Dirk asked.

"Anything."

Wire pulled the big digital camera from its case and began taking pictures of the cove, dictating to Maeve so she could label the shots: "Facing out to sea." *Click.* "Facing north." *Click.* "Facing south." *Click.* "Type in the GPS coordinates with these shots, would you? See the little logo for that?"

"Got it," Maeve affirmed.

*First time I've seen her act serious for any length of time*, Wire realized. *She's really getting into this.*

"How can you act so calm?" Grizz sounded curious. "I just keep thinking—that's someone's father or husband or best friend. It gives me the willies. And you two young people are acting like—like this is some kind of science project."

"Crime Scene Club has taught us well," Wire replied. "This *is* a science project. But not because we don't care, but so we can achieve justice for the victim. If you get all emotional, that helps no one. But if we can focus, stay objective, then there's much more chance we'll find out who did this and why."

"Actually," Maeve gave a ghoulish grin, "I kind of dig creepy stuff."

Wire shook his head. "I want to get the highest view I can of the victim and the area around him." He pulled a tall tripod out of the case and quickly switched lenses.

"Got a way to establish scale?" Maeve asked.

"There's a ruler in the case there. Can you drop it real careful-like a few feet out from the body?"

"Can do."

"All right, this looks good. Not ninety degrees but best we can do under the circumstances." Wire clicked away.

"Trying flash and non-flash?" Maeve suggested.

"Roger."

"You guys act like real professionals." Wire detected no insincerity in Grizz's tone.

"We've investigated four criminal cases," Maeve replied proudly.

"That how you got those scars on your legs and chest?" Dirk asked.

*That guy's got a lot of nerve*, Wire thought, but Maeve was unfazed.

"Got these on our second case," she said, like a soldier boasting about battle wounds. "The perp sabotaged my brother's sports car—which I drove off a cliff."

"Gnarly." The surfer boy was clearly impressed.

Wire took the camera off its tripod and walked around the body in a clockwise motion, about five feet away, taking shots at each angle of the circumference.

"Do those look sharp enough?" he asked Maeve, who stared at each shot on the screen of the PDA.

"Hard to tell—sun's glaring onto the display, but I think they're good," she answered.

"Okay, I'm going to move in closer now. I'll have to leave tracks in the sand all around the body, but I already documented the larger scene."

"Go for it."

Wire changed lenses again and repeated his circular path around the dead swimmer, this time much closer, taking shots from each angle up and down the entire length of the corpse.

"Got good pics of that wound on his forehead?" Maeve asked.

"Getting them now. I'll get in super-close-up and take them from a variety of angles." The camera made a constant *swoosh-click* noise as Wire's finger busily went up and down on the shutter button.

"Hey, you wanted us to look for stuff—does this count?" Dirk reached down toward a empty soda can, half-buried by sand.

"Yes, but—hey, don't *touch* it!"

"What do ya want me to do?"

"There's a pair of tweezers in the case, and a paper bag. Wait until I take a picture of its location, then label it and put it in the bag—without touching it. It's probably not related to this case, but on the other hand it might be useful DNA evidence."

"Why do we have to do all that?" Dirk looked peeved.

"Don't you ever watch CSI?"

"That the show with the older blond chick?"

*This guy's really low on the evolutionary scale. He must have the brains of a slug*, Wire thought.

"Just do what Wire says," Grizz told his protégé. "I don't know who this poor devil is, but he was a fellow surfer—you can tell by his build and his gear. We gotta do what we can to find out what happened to him—and these kids from Arizona obviously know how."

Dirk snarled but complied.

"Got pictures of the surfboard and the strappy thing?" Maeve asked.

"You mean the *leash*," Dirk corrected.

"I've gotta put a new card in the camera and I'll get the board and leash, close-up and from all angles," Wire agreed.

"Tide's comin' under the guy," Grizz noticed. "He'll be floating again soon."

"I know we're not supposed to change anything," Maeve said, "but the ocean's changing the scene anyway. Think we should turn him over and get shots of his front side?"

"I suppose so," Wire replied, "but I don't want to touch him. Seems kinda . . . wrong, and . . . creepy."

Grizz grinned at him. "So even you young ghouls have your limits?"

But Maeve was already slipping on gloves. In her bikini with tattooed bats flocking across her back, she didn't look much like what you'd expect of a crime scene investigator, Wire thought. *But she's really good at this.* She squatted beside the body and pulled hard, rolling him onto his back. "Better get close-ups of that gash from this angle."

Grizz shook his head at the dark-haired girl. "I still don't know how you kids do it. I've seen big-wave surfers who didn't have that much guts."

"Someone has to do this," Wire replied, "or this guy's case will never get solved. I'd rather let the local cops do their job, believe me. But since they're not here. . . ."

"How many pictures do you have to take?" Dirk asked.

"Lots," Maeve replied. "Especially since the Neptune PD is so slow arriving on the scene."

Twenty minutes later, two police officers made their way down the path to the cove, a tall man with blond hair and bronzed skin and a smartly dressed woman. "Looks like a surfing accident," the man stated with an air of certainty.

"You sure?" Grizz asked him.

"Yep. Coroner will be here soon. We'll guard the body in the meantime."

"We have pictures of the scene," Maeve offered.

The man turned a quizzical face her direction. "Who are you?"

"We're with the Crime Scene Club of Flagstaff Charter School," Wire explained. "We've been trained to properly document a crime scene."

"That's nice. You kids can run along now," the officer replied.

"But—you'll want the documentation we just did," Maeve suggested.

"I can burn them onto a flash drive with my PDA," Wire added.

"Thank you, we'd appreciate that," the female officer said, apparently trying to be the "good cop" of the pair.

The male officer's face was stoic behind his shaded eyeglasses.

A few minutes later, the CSC teens, along with Dirk and Grizz, headed back up the path. Jessa rejoined them, saying, "Sorry I couldn't be much help back there. I wasn't feeling so hot."

"No apology needed," Maeve told her.

"Would you like a drink? I have some Gatorade in the van," Dirk offered.

*The slug can be chivalrous*, Wire noted.

"Wish those officers would take their job seriously," Grizz fumed. "You teens acted a hundred times more professional than they did."

# Chapter 3
# BAD COMPANY

By the time the three CSC teens drove back to their hotel, stopping for lunch on the way and a couple of shopping diversions for the girls, it was late afternoon. Wire remembered the way back and was glad he didn't have to fight the girls to help with navigation. Detective Kwan still wasn't feeling well, but she insisted on meeting the three in the lobby to discuss the morning's adventure.

The detective looked a little haggard, but she was dressed professionally as always. After hearing their report, she phoned the Neptune morgue for an update. The secretary there said the autopsy was in progress, and he would call when it was finished.

"Maybe we should ask the two men you met this morning—Grizz and Dirk?—if they would drive over and discuss the case with us," Miss Kwan suggested.

"Right on," Maeve agreed.

"What do we need them for?" Wire asked, irritated. "They don't know anything about criminal investigation or science or—anything."

"But Dirk's kinda cute." Jessa was smiling in a stupid, dreamy sort of way.

"Cute like a pit bull," Wire countered. "We're better off discussing this without them."

"We could vote on it," Maeve suggested.

Wire sighed. "Never mind, invite the beach bums over."

While Maeve pulled out her cell phone to call Grizz and Dirk, Wire tried again to reach QT on his PDA. She wasn't logged on. He also tried to phone her, but no one answered. *What's going on with her? She's the only reason I came on this lame excuse for a vacation.*

Detective Kwan suggested Wire bring his laptop to the lounge and transfer all the pictures onto it for easy viewing. A half hour later, Grizz pulled his rusty bus in front of the hotel.

"Nice place—has genuine atmosphere," the older man noted as he looked around the hotel lounge.

Wire wasn't so thrilled with the Surfside Hotel. *Nice atmosphere for roaches. And their wireless service totally sucks, they only have basic channels, and the air-conditioning units are older than I am.* In his opinion, the glass floats, rough-hewn outrigger canoe, and other items of nautical décor in the lobby weren't much use.

Grizz turned to Detective Kwan. "Aloha, I don't believe we've met."

"Dorothy Kwan, Flagstaff Arizona PD. I sponsor the club for these young people." Wire was surprised the policewoman offered her first name.

"Grizz Sanchez, owner of Grizzly Surf shop, at your service, ma'am. And this is Dirk Hayden," he added, "my apprentice in the shaping business and a rising talent on the waves."

"Grizz here is the real talent," the young man demurred. "He's a freakin' legend—some folks say he learned surfing from Duke Kahanamoku."

The grey-haired man laughed. "I'm not *that* old—but I did shake his hand once, just before he died. I have hung out with Corky Carrol and Bruce Brown, though," he added, "and Kelly Slater used one of my boards." Wire noticed that Detective Kwan was unimpressed; clearly, the names didn't mean anything more to her than they did to him. Grizz looked a little disappointed. "Any word on our mysterious body?"

"I called the Neptune coroner's office," she replied. "They are doing the autopsy, and— Hold on, my cell's buzzing, that's them now." She answered the phone and listened, nodding.

"Well?" Jessa asked when she flipped the phone shut.

"Nothing you didn't already guess," Ms. Kwan said. "The deceased is a Caucasian male, mid-thirties, blue eyes and blond hair, in excellent health prior to his death."

"They have a name for him?" Jessa wanted to know.

"No ID yet. They've gone over missing person reports—no one matches this guy's description. He's just John Doe for now. He died of a blow to the forehead—that visible mark you photographed—

and apparently drifted four or five hours after death. They're ruling it an accident, probably concussion from his own board or perhaps rocks in the water."

Grizz shook his head. "That was no accident."

"But coroners know their stuff—why would they mistake the COD?" Wire argued.

"The what?"

"Cause of death."

Grizz looked thoughtful. "There's a lotta weird stuff goes down in Neptune. Word is everyone from the mayor to the police chief is crooked. I wouldn't be surprised if someone slipped a couple of g's to that suit who was back at the cove and said, 'There's a body in the cove—and it's an accident, got that?' He said, 'Sure,' and that's why the detective didn't even look at the body when he finally arrived at the scene."

Wire grinned. "Conspiracy theories are a dime a dozen. Half the guys on the Internet are full of theories: UFOs and Atlantis and shadow organizations running the world. But crazy talk's no substitute for science. I'll put my money on the coroner's decision."

"There are wacky conspiracy theories all right," Ms. Kwan interjected, "but sometimes in crime work there are real conspiracies covering up the truth. And, sorry to say, not all police departments are as much on the up-and-up as ours is. Let's look at the documentation from the site."

Wire grudgingly tapped a key to play a slideshow of his photographs from the crime scene.

"What about those footprints there?" Detective Kwan asked.

"That's me—I ran up to check if the man needed first aid," Grizz explained.

"Hmm. Looks like he drifted into shore, consistent with the coroner's report."

The slide show shuffled pictures; now the computer screen showed the ugly gash on the head of the corpse. "Hold it," Ms. Kwan ordered. Wire tapped another key and froze the picture.

"I don't know much about rocks in the ocean," the detective commented, "but that doesn't look like a wound caused by a natural object."

"Nope. It's too clean," Grizz agreed.

"Knife wound?" Maeve offered.

"No, not deep enough, and too wide," Ms. Kwan replied. "It doesn't look like anything I'm familiar with. What about that surfboard fin?"

"It happens all the time," Dirk explained. "You wipe out, the board goes up in the air, catches on the leash, comes down and—wham!"

"Does that kill people?" Jessa asked.

"I've seen folks knocked out," the young man told her. "Leaves a mark like this," and he pulled back a strand of his long red hair revealing a scar, several inches long, at the top of his forehead.

"Oh, you poor thing." Jessa oozed sympathy.

"That's nothing. You wanna see my shark bite?"

"Not today," Detective Kwan interrupted, "we have serious business." She looked toward the older surfer. "What do you think, Grizz? Could that injury be from the fin of his surfboard?"

"Depends on the board, I guess. If it was an old solid balsa board, with a monster skeg on it, and the waves were really big—I suppose that could happen. I didn't look closely at his stick, more concerned with the body. You got pictures of the board?"

Wire tapped at his notebook, and the red board became visible.

"It's a thruster," Dirk offered, "real thin and light."

"The only way you could get enough force to make that wound would be to hold the board and smash it hard onto the guy's head," Grizz said. "And that would break the stick nearly in half. Let's go slowly over those pics of the board. See any cracks?"

They didn't.

"Hey!" Dirk suddenly cried, "where's the sex wax?"

"I beg your pardon!" Detective Kwan looked startled.

Dirk grinned. "Surfers rub their board down with wax, let the sun melt it, and rub sand in for traction," he explained.

Grizz nodded. "Weird thing is—this board's perfectly clean, like it's never been used. Nice observation, Dirk."

*The slug might have a rudimentary brain, after all*, Wire reluctantly admitted to himself.

"What's that mark, there?" Jessa pointed to a picture of the board.

"Well, well, it's made by WaveTech," Dirk chuckled.

"You know them?" Detective Kwan asked.

"They're our competition," Grizz explained. "They pour their boards—totally non-traditional."

"Do they sell many like this?"

"Not too many," Dirk answered. "Most folks can't afford them. And Grizz is right— they're lacking lateral strength, so if that board did the damage on Mystery Man's forehead, it would be toast."

"Would WaveTech have records of their customers? Perhaps we can ID our body through their sales receipts," the policewoman suggested.

"They won't want to talk to me," Grizz explained, "since I stole their poster girl—Keisha. But if you called, they might be willing to cooperate." He scratched his head. "This is strange. Our mysterious corpse was probably a hardcore surfer, or he wouldn't own a pricey stick like that. But he didn't wax it down—which makes no sense for someone that knows the sport. He died from a blow to the head, but it wasn't his board and it wasn't a rock in the water. And the Neptune City officials just brush over all these oddities and stamp 'accident' on their report. I doubt they even looked at the corpse. I'm telling you, there's a mystery here—and I daresay a cold-blooded crime as well."

"Oh crap." Wire clutched his hair in his fists.

"What?"

"I just remembered—I left the tripod on the beach."

"If it's worth anything, it's gone," Dirk told him.

"Maybe the tide covered it for most of the day. I have to go back and look for it." Wire was so angry with himself that he could hear his voice shake, which only added to his outrage.

"It's not like you to forget things," Detective Kwan observed.

"I'll drive back and find it." Wire snapped his laptop shut, and reached for the keys to the rental van.

"Better hurry, it'll be dark soon," Grizz cautioned.

"We never got to surf—maybe we could try skinny-dipping when it gets dark." Maeve grinned and got to her feet.

Wire shook his head at her. *I can never tell if she's serious or not.*

"I'll go with you too," Jessa added.

"Me too!" Dirk was practically drooling over Jessa, Wire thought.

"You going with the kids?" Grizz asked Detective Kwan.

"I still don't feel so good—something I ate last night keeping my stomach queasy. I'll stay here and think a little more about this mystery."

"I'll keep you company," Grizz told her, "if you don't mind."

"No, that would be nice and—I could use your help," she added quickly. "I think we should work with one of these facial shots. Restore color, cover over the wound. If we can create a lifelike digital image of the man and put it on posters, someone in the area might recognize who he is."

"But the Neptune coroner said there's no case. How we going to get around that?"

"There is no case. And I'm just an off-duty officer here on vacation—officially. But that doesn't mean a few of us concerned citizens can't ask questions around town."

On the long drive down to Neptune, the two girls sat in the back of the van with Dirk, listening to the kid telling tall tales of his macho exploits. Wire kept to himself, pretending to concentrate on his driving. Finally, they reached the place where they had parked that morning; it seemed like a long time ago now. One other car was in the parking lot now: an old Dodge Charger, painted sparkling maroon and lowered to the ground.

"You go ahead," Dirk told the others. "I just wanna be alone a few minutes." Wire noted the rectangular shape in the boy's pants pocket, and he was pretty sure he knew why Dirk wanted to be alone. *Solitude and cigarettes, oh yeah. Figures he'd be into a disgusting habit like that.*

Wire, Maeve, and Jessa walked down the trail through the gathering dusk. For an odd instant, Wire imagined they might come upon another body, washed up on the sand—but nothing like that happened. Instead, they saw four stocky young men, dressed all in black and white, wearing baggy shirts, long t-shirts, hair nets, and bandanas. They were seated on folding chairs around a small fire, and a pile of beer bottles lay strewn around them.

Wire hoped to avoid their attention but failed.

"Hey—this is our beach," one of the guys called.

"Uh, sorry. I left some equipment here this morning," Wire explained. "I'll just look for a minute and be gone."

"You mean, 'please,' don't you, dork? You don't *tell* us what you're gonna do. Ya gotta *ask* real nice—'cause Loco Motion rules this beach."

"Loco Motion?"

"What, you never heard of us? That's messed." One of them jumped up.

Wire took a step backward. "I'm not from here. We're from Arizona."

"Hey, cowgirls! Wanna go for a ride?" another of the Locos shouted at Maeve and Jessa.

"Forget it, fatty," Maeve replied without batting an eye.

*Bad idea. Speak nicely to these guys.*

All four of the toughs were on their feet now, cat-calling and making rude gestures toward the girls.

"Ooh, I'm feelin' hungry for Wonder Bread tonight."

"The Goth chick's mine, boys."

"In your dreams, rat-face," Maeve yelled.

*She's being so not smart. . . .* Wire was sweating, despite the cool ocean breeze.

The four guys walked rapidly toward the CSC teens, spreading out as they drew closer.

*I don't have a snowball's chance, but I've got to try and protect the girls*, Wire told himself. He pushed his chest forward, tried to look formidable. "Leave us alone!" His voice came out shriller than he intended.

They laughed.

"Look at the little boy gettin' all bad."

"Whatcha say, dork?"

"We gonna smoke you."

*Phoomp!* Wire never knew what hit him.

Hot wet liquid poured from his nose. Dimly, he heard laughter, then Jessa's voice: "Get your filthy hands off me!"

*Gotta do something. Gotta draw them away from the girls.* He straightened, gasping, ribs burning. *I'm smarter than they are*, he assured himself. *I can do this.* He staggered a few steps down the beach, the opposite direction from where the four thugs were dragging the girls. "Hey! I'm not done with you yet!" he yelled.

They looked back at him and burst out laughing. "You really want more?"

*Wham!* A hard object hit the back of his head. He went face down in the sand. A booted heel shoved his mouth into the coarse grit.

Wire struggled to raise his head. His glasses were crushed and sandy, giving everything a fog-like appearance.

"Let go of me, you baboon!" One of the guys reeled backward as Jessa shot a can of pepper spray directly into his face.

"Aiee!" Maeve let out a blood-curdling yell and sent a lightning-quick kick into the groin of another attacker, followed by a chop to his head. He doubled over.

Through his clouded spectacles, Wire watched helplessly as a bigger assailant grabbed Jessa from behind, pinning her arms behind her back. Wire had never been all that sure if he believed in God—but he prayed now, desperately, to whomever might be listening: *Help us! Please!*

"Aaagh!" Jessa's attacker suddenly released her, clutching at his back.

The next instant, Wire saw Dirk slamming both fists into the Loco. The guy went down, but two of the others leapt at the red-haired boy. Wire could barely make out what was happening through his broken lenses, but when the dust settled, all four of the attackers lay groaning in the sand. Jessa and Maeve stood beside Dirk, grinning.

"Now listen up, vatos—this is no way to treat the ladies," Dirk told them. One of the fallen men moaned. "I want you to say 'sorry' to these girls."

"Sorry, *chicas*," one of the Locos muttered.

"Louder—I can't hear you." Dirk put his toe gently on the guy's ribs.

"Sorry!"

"That's better." Dirk turned to Wire. "Hey, geek, can you walk?"

Wire coughed, tried not to gag, and then pulled himself painfully upright. "My name's Wire," he muttered, spitting sad from his mouth.

"Whatever. Whaddya say? I think we'd better get going. I'm not seeing no tripod around here."

They started back up the path out of the cove, but then Dirk turned back toward the Loco Motion members. "Hey, you guys know anything about a body that turned up here this morning?"

"What?" The guy shook his head. "You on crack?"

Dirk walked over to the prone young man and grasped his baggy shorts, pulling them up into a painful wedgie. The guy yelped.

"Tell me what you know," Dirk said calmly,.

"I give it to ya straight." Another Loco, wearing a black bandana, sat up and answered Dirk. "Word is he drowned. We don't know nuthin' else. But I tell ya—if we'da offed him, he wouldn't look near so pretty when we was done."

Dirk nodded and headed back up the path with the others. "Don't look back," he whispered. "Can't let them see fear. They're like wild dogs that way."

Wire gasped for breath, clutched his side, and stumbled upward.

"You need to be more careful," Dirk told the CSC teens. "This isn't the boonies anymore. You need a watchdog around if you're gonna mess with these bad boys."

"Wire, you were totally brave." Maeve patted his shoulder.

"Ouch. Thank you for noticing."

"Yeah, you really tried to save us," Jessa said.

*Tried. Thanks a lot.*

"Think they're telling the truth about the corpse?" Maeve whispered to Dirk.

"They're filthy liars. Don't trust Locos any further than I can spit," he replied. "But what that guy said at the end—that makes sense. If Loco Motion decides to hurt someone—they're not very subtle about it."

An hour later, the three had dropped Dirk off at his Huntington Beach apartment and were driving back to their hotel.

"Dirk's awful cute," Maeve commented.

"I could go for him, but . . . I've had awful luck with men," Jessa replied.

"That baboon?" Wire couldn't believe his ears. "I don't know what you two see in him."

"I do believe Wire is jealous," Jessa chuckled.

"Me, jealous of that brainless beach boy? He couldn't think his way out of a pay toilet. Bet he doesn't even own a computer."

*Just wait. I'll show Dirk and Grizz how to solve a crime, Wire thought. Those testosterone-laden surf snobs will see how much more you can do with brains than with brawn.*

# Chapter 4
# "I KNOW THAT GUY"

The next morning, Grizz dusted down the cases at Grizzly Surf Shop. Dirk swept the corners of the store.

"Why you got that hood on?" Grizz asked his employee.

"Gotta keep my reputation up," the younger man told him.

"I thought we were gonna work on *changing* your reputation," Grizz suggested quietly.

Dirk changed the subject. "Can you believe that geek, Wire? If I hadn't saved his scrawny butt, the Loco Motion boys would've made fish bait out of him."

"You're too hard on the guy. He's got a good aura around him—I can see it."

"There you go again, gettin' all mystical."

"There's more to the world than what meets your eye."

"Enlighten me, oh great Obi Wan."

Grizz shook his head. "Just watch—that young man is going to solve this mystery. I'll bet you fifty dollars."

"Bet for real?"

"For real."

"You're on, old man."

"Hold it. You don't have fifty bucks to your name."

"You can take it out of my paycheck."

"It's a bet." The two exchanged shaka signs.

"By the way," Dirk asked, "how come you're so interested in that stiff in the cove?"

"He's not 'a stiff,' he's your bro."

"I don't have a brother."

"Yes, you do—hundreds of brothers. There used to be kinship between surfers—and hopefully your generation will reforge that bond."

"There you go gettin' mystical again."

"I can't help thinking about that guy on the beach," Grizz said more somberly. "I don't know his name, but I'll bet he loved surfing and sunsets and pretty women, just like any other guy does. Now he's lying cold and still in the morgue and he's crying out—but silently, so most folks can't hear him. But I hear him, saying, 'Don't let them cover up my death. Something awful happened to me—and you've got to let the world know about it.'"

"Whoa." The young man put his hands up. "Thought you quit smoking pot."

"I did. Stuff wouldn't let me see straight. Now I'm off it, I see more than most folks do—I see beyond the physical realm into what is."

"Shall we try and levitate today, oh great Jedi Master?"

Grizz just shook his head. He knew Dirk loved him like a father, but the teen refused to take the his spiritual thoughts seriously.

The door chimed as a lanky man entered the shop, his skin darkened by the sun, long scraggly hair hanging off his shoulders.

"Hey, Terrapin, what's happenin'?" Grizz asked.

"Broke my board down in Mexico. Need a new stick—but it's gotta be just right. You're the only one I trust to make it for me, Grizz."

"I aim to please. Just tell me what you want." Grizz grabbed a notepad, then paused. "Hey, you still live down near Neptune?"

"Got a shack in Neptune, right near the cove."

"Don't suppose you could tell me who this dude is?" Grizz pulled out the enhanced photo of the man found on the beach.

"I know that guy—Joe Nui. He lives in La Jolla, but comes up coast to surf Neptune Cove. Say, he doesn't look so good in that picture. Is Joe okay?"

Grizz hesitated; now that he knew the guy's name, he felt an even closer tie to this unfortunate soul. "He's dead, Terrapin."

"Shoot. What happened?"

"Neptune PD say he died from an accident surfing. But we saw his body. I'm not so sure it was accidental."

The lanky man shook his head. "Man, that sucks, dude. How's Brandee taking it?"

"Brandee?"

"Joe's wife—Brandee Zam."

"*The* Brandee Zam?" Dirk shouted from the side of the store. "The chick that sang, 'Wham, Zam—you're my man'?"

"Yep. That's his wife. You didn't know they were married?"

"We didn't know who the poor fellow was—not until you identified him just now," Grizz explained. "And I'm sure his wife doesn't know he's dead either. I'll call the Neptune PD and they'll tell her."

"Sad." Terrapin shook his head. "That'll just make her worse."

"What happened to her, anyway?" Dirk wanted to know. "She was real famous when I was in junior high—one smokin' hot chick, with her picture all over and songs on the radio and Internet. I haven't even heard of her since. It's like she disappeared."

"She got into all the wrong stuff," Terrapin told him. "Drugs, alcohol, all sorts of nutty behavior. The record companies dropped her. She lost her talent and became an embarrassment. Then she met up with Joe and started to settle down. But last I talked to him, poor Joe said she was falling back into her addictions. As if he needed more troubles."

"Wait a minute." A light suddenly flashed in Grizz's head. "Joe Nui—he used to live in Santa Cruz, a decade ago. He did a few tours on the pro circuit, sponsored by Body Glove."

"Yep. That's Joe."

"What happened to him after that?"

Terrapin sighed. "Like a lot of dudes that get all excited about goin' pro, he didn't make it professionally, and he couldn't be happy working for some guy behind a desk. He was livin' like a bum, until he met Brandee. After they married, he lived off her money—till she ran out. Then he borrowed dough." Terrapin shrugged. "All he really wanted to do was surf. Couldn't seem to find his place outside the ocean."

"Did you say he owed people money?" Grizz asked.

"Sure did."

"Who?"

"Pretty much everybody around Oceanside—and some folks in Neptune."

"Big amounts?"

"He owes, well, I guess I should say, he *owed* me four grand. But I was never sore about it, figured it was my way to support a fellow soul surfer. Guy like Nui, you couldn't stay mad at him for long. He was a mess, but he was real, you know? Never understood why he hitched up with a high-maintenance Hollywood broad like Brandee Zam."

Dirk looked thoughtful. "I don't suppose he owed the Loco Motion gang money?"

"Afraid he did," Terrapin replied. "Pretty scary, huh?"

Grizz blinked the moisture out of his eyes. "Terrapin, you've been more help today than you'd ever imagine. It's good karma brought you here. I have to make a few calls. Would you mind giving Dirk here the specs for your new stick? He's turning into a great shaper—someday he'll surpass me."

Grizz walked through the workshop behind his store and stepped outside into the alley, where he leaned back against the wall. *Another soul enslaved by that faithless goddess the ocean. And then he married a real-life goddess, Brandee Zam. Now she's fallen apart and he's gone from this earth. Well, gotta call the Neptune PD. They can inform the widow, and hopefully they'll have sense to talk with the Loco Motion gang about this. And then . . . guess maybe I'll call Dorothy Kwan and update the Crime Scene Club.*

He pulled a handkerchief from his pocket and dabbed at his eyes, then produced a cigarette from another pocket along with a pack of matches. He lit up and took a drag. *Poor Joe Nui.*

*Another lousy day in paradise.*

Wire had just finished straightening and cleaning his wire-rimmed eyeglasses; thankfully, there was no permanent damage. The girls wanted to spend the morning watching soap operas in their room, doing makeup, and who knows what other girly things. Ms. Kwan was either recuperating or brooding over the crime—Wire couldn't tell which. There was still no word from QT, a fact that tied his heart up in knots. And every time he moved, he felt aches and pains from the night before. *Mental note: at all costs, avoid meeting Loco Motion again.*

The day started looking better, though, after he persuaded Ms. Kwan to let him take the rental car and drive to Beverly Hills by himself, where he could visit the Spy Store and enjoy a few hours browsing gadgets. He was in the van, pulling away from the hotel, when a call came on his Bluetooth.

"Change of plans; new developments in our mystery. Meet us in the lobby."

*Maybe there is a Deity after all*, Wire thought, *and this trip is its way of punishing me for something I did wrong.*

No sooner had he entered the hotel door, when Jessa called out, "We know who the vic is—and you won't believe who he's married to!"

They filled him in, and Wire scratched his head. "So he was married to the cheesiest wannabe singer of the past decade. Are you sure the guy didn't kill himself? Because if I was married to Brandee Zam, that's what I'd do."

"That's a terrible thing to say," Jessa scolded. "She has a very fine voice and some clever choreography in her videos."

"Can we get back on track?" Detective Kwan asked. "I called Neptune PD for an update. I'm afraid they aren't very enthused about cooperating with me, which makes me wonder if Mr. Sanchez's misgivings about that department may be on-target. Anyway, they've informed Ms. Zam of her husband's death, but they haven't interviewed her yet—something about jurisdiction, since she lives in La Jolla. They promised they'll talk to the Loco Motion gang about Mr. Nui's demise, but I'm skeptical they'll pursue that very far. Officially, they are still saying 'accidental death while surfing.'"

"Tell him about my idea, Ms. Kwan. Tell Wire what we're gonna do!" Jessa bounced up and down on the lobby couch.

"At Jessa's suggestion I've called Brandee Zam, explained that we're not working officially since there is no formal case, but maybe with our expertise we can help her learn more about her husband's death."

"And she agreed to see us!" Jessa beamed.

*I'm missing the Spy Store to go see Brandee Zam?*

Ms. Kwan decided she was in shape now to drive. The girls sat in the back, giggling, and Wire sat shotgun, talking to Ms. Kwan as she drove.

"We only have three more days in California. What can we hope to achieve in that time?" Wire asked the detective.

"I doubt we'll solve anything, but we can do work that might help the local PD."

"They're not admitting this is any kind of crime, though."

"Maybe they will if we turn up some more evidence."

Brandee Zam lived in a palatial mass of stone and glass, surrounded by faux Greek statues and modern sculpture. *This is the worst architectural mess I've ever seen*, Wire thought. Even Jessa, apparently a fan of Brandee, had to admit the mansion was somewhat lacking in taste. It did, however, have a magnificent cliff-side view of the ocean.

After the gate guard admitted them onto the grounds, the CSC parked their van, and a servant ushered them into the mansion itself. "Ms. Zam will be with you shortly," he told them. They sat waiting in huge leather couches beside a picture-window view of the Pacific.

"I thought Grizz's friend said she was running out of money," Maeve whispered to Ms. Kwan. "It doesn't look like she's downgraded her lifestyle."

"I suppose everything is relative," the detective replied.

"You must be the detective and kids from Air-iz-zhoona," a husky female voice exclaimed.

Wire blinked. He hardly recognized Brandee Zam. He had a mental image of her as glamorous, sexy to the nth degree, a sparkling blond in body-clinging sequin outfits and fantastically permed hairdos. The woman before him was arguably the same person: in her late twenties, blond, and still possessing a not-unpleasant figure. But she was garbed in a thick fleece nightgown and slippers, her eyes baggy and unfocused, her hair disheveled—the furthest thing from glamorous.

Brandee plopped herself onto an empty couch and sprawled back on it. "I can't believe Joe is dead," she said in a slurred voice. "It's shuch an awful shock. I haven't been myself shince hearing the news."

"Do you mind if we ask you some questions? We're hoping to learn something more about this terrible tragedy—and maybe that will help you to be more at rest." Detective Kwan's voice was businesslike but sympathetic.

"Oh, please asshk. Nice of you to care. But . . . it was an accshident." Brandee turned to her servant, who hovered near the door. "Biff, could you please... I need something to steady my nerves."

The servant nodded and glided away.

*The only thing that would steady this lady's nerves would be three months in rehab*, Wire thought.

"What makes you so sure it was an accident?" Detective Kwan asked.

"That's what the po-leesh said."

"Could they possibly be mistaken?"

"He left this, the night before . . . they found him." Brandee handed detective Kwan a piece of paper. Wire leaned over to read the handwriting:

*Brandee, gone moonlight surfing.*
*Joe.*

"Biff! Where's my drink?" the celebrity shouted. The servant reappeared and handed her a glass filled with some concoction that she quickly emptied. Then she turned her attention back to the Crime Scene Club. "Poor Joe was so depresshed. . . . I wonder if he just decided to end it all? The only . . . the only . . . uh . . . con-so-laashun is that he died shuurfing. He . . . loved to shuurf."

"Is there anyone who might have wanted to hurt him?" Ms. Kwan asked.

Brandee started to laugh—and continued chuckling for what seemed to Wire a very long and inappropriate time. She caught her breath, motioned to the servant to refill her glass, and said, "Only half the people in shouthern California. Joe owed everyone money."

"That's odd. You don't appear badly off," Wire said bluntly.

"Joe was ir-reesponshable. He needed to learn to sha-port hisself. So I quit giving him money. And . . . I did have some hard times fi-nan-shally, but

I've been more . . . forshunate lately." Brandee stood suddenly, then lost her balance and fell backward onto the couch. "I don't feel well. Time for you to go." She waved at them with a shooing motion.

Ms. Kwan handed her a card. "If you think of anything you want to tell us about your husband's death, you can call us at the number written on the back."

"Shank you. You're very kind."

Detective Kwan shook her head as they drove away. "No help there."

It was hard to believe that the celebrated singer Wire had seen on television could turn into someone so clueless. *She's either the most pathetic soul I've ever met*, he mused, *or the best actress.*

# Chapter 5
# CHANGING PRIORITIES

That evening, Grizz sat by himself at a dimly lit table in Trader Tom's Tiki Paradise. The old restaurant evoked a mood both adventurous and creepy; it was a good match for Grizz's state of mind. He stared at the big fish swimming in an aquarium by the wall that was rumored to be more than five decades old. *Wish it could tell us everything it's seen, staring out from behind those glass walls.*

The waitress came over. "Your drink, sir."

Grizz thanked her, and then his gaze drifted over to a life-sized carving of a hula girl; for some reason, it made him think of Dorothy Kwan. *She's a sweet thing*, he mused, but then other women came to mind, his former wives and girlfriends. Over the years, Grizz had mastered the complex wave patterns and currents of the ocean, but he somehow always failed to comprehend the vagaries of the opposite sex.

An nasal voice interrupted his thoughts. "Mr. Grizz, I believe I have some items that may interest you."

A short, balding man with enormous bulging eyes pulled up a chair next to him and slid three manila envelopes across the table. Grizz instinctively backed away. The photographer Peter Lonnie was notorious up and down the California coast; the guy would sell compromising pictures of his own mother given enough hard cash. But Grizz forced himself to sit still. *Fate has its reasons—even for unpleasant encounters*, he reminded himself.

"I understand you are interested in the ah . . . most unfortunate death of Joe Nui." Peter Lonnie spoke with a vaguely foreign accent that gave his words a strange, slippery sound.

"Who told you that?"

"Oh, Mr. Grizz, you understand, I am sure, that we professionals cannot divulge our sources. It would not be honorable."

*Not much honor at the bottom of the cesspool last I checked.* "All right, Lonnie, what do you have to show me?"

"As you know sir, I am an esteemed photographer of famous persons—such as Miss Brandee Zam—as well as those who are close to them, such as the late Mr. Nui."

"Cut the flowery talk. Get to it."

Lonnie looked irritated. "I have photos that might be of great help to someone interested in the real story of Mr. Nui's demise."

"How much?"

"Must we talk about money? Surely a little cash is of no consequence when facing the mysteries of life and death, do you not agree?"

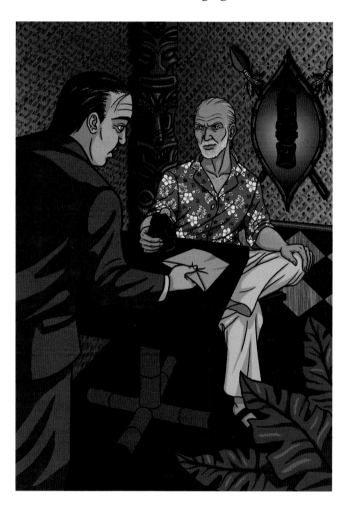

Grizz glared at the toad-like figure. Lonnie put up his hands.

"This first picture is the least valuable of the bunch. I would willingly part from it—despite the effort of attaining such a rare image—for only fifty dollars."

The surfer's eyes narrowed; he wavered between kicking the little weasel out from his table and buying the envelope. At last, he reached into his pocket, pulled out two bills, and thrust them in front of Lonnie. "I'll give you forty."

"Mr. Grizz, special for you."

He opened the envelope and pulled out a picture of a man crouched on his surfboard, coming out of a curl.

Grizz let out a hiss of annoyance. "You rat—I could've got this picture out of any old surf mag."

"Oh no, sir. I shot this one myself, just a year ago. Notice the excellent focus, the clarity of Mr. Nui's face."

Grizz was seething. He expected some big revelation, not an ordinary sports shot. And then it hit him: "Nui was a goofy foot!"

"Mr. Grizz has found something interesting in my picture?"

"The guy surfed right foot forward, but when his body washed up, the board was tethered to his right foot—when it should have been his left, like in this picture." Even in the dark of the tiki bar, the picture clearly showed a leash strapped to the surfer's left ankle.

"Ah, you see? My assistance is already valuable. And that, Mr. Grizz, is the *least* interesting of these images that I am offering you."

"Will you stop calling me 'Mr. Grizz?' It annoys me."

"Sincere apologies, kind sir. I do not mean to offend, it's just that despite years of living in this wonderful country, I sometimes—"

"Stow it. What's in this envelope?"

"Unfortunately, I have learned over years of professional experience not to promise exact details until a transaction is—"

"How much?"

"One hundred dollars. A trifle, I am sure you will agree, after—"

Grizz clenched and unclenched his fist, reached again for his wallet, and dropped a small stack of bills in front of Peter Lonnie.

The paparazzi counted quickly. "This is only eighty-seven dollars."

"All I have. Take it or leave it."

"For someone of such honorable reputation as yourself, and since I always seek to be generous. . ."

Grizz tore open the envelope. Inside was a picture of Joe Nui, in shorts and a t-shirt, talking to a clean-shaven, dark-haired man in an overcoat. "What is this?"

"That gentleman in the suit is Guido Zarducci."

"Who?"

"You do not know of Mr. Zarducci? I expect your devotion to the waves does not permit you to stay fully informed of the news. Perhaps you should ask your detective friend. . . ."

"How do you know so much about my life?"

"As I said, most kind sir, I am a professional investigator of sorts myself, and I have my sources, which, regrettably, must remain—"

Grizz had had enough. He stood, looking for the waitress so he could pay for his drink and leave.

"But Mr. Grizz?" Lonnie plucked at his sleeve. "You have not asked about the third picture."

Grizz shrugged off his hand. "Waitress!"

"For every mystery, there is a missing piece of the puzzle," Lonnie persisted, "a fact that completes the entire picture . . . that makes the incomprehensible obvious."

Despite his dislike of the guy, Grizz was interested. "What's your price?"

"One thousand dollars exactly. No reduced price this time, Mr. Grizz."

"Too much. No way."

"The image in this last envelope could fetch even more than that. There are people who would pay handsomely to see this—or to make sure it is *not* seen by certain other parties. I have heard many good things about you, and that is why I am offering this at such a bargain. . ."

The waitress came over and Grizz handed her his credit card. "Ring me outta here quick." She nodded and hurried away.

Lonnie pressed a business card into Grizz's hand. "Take this . . . in case you change your mind. Anytime you call, I shall be there at your convenience. Assuming, of course, that the picture has not been sold to some other interested persons."

The waitress handed Grizz his credit card and he started for the door. Behind him, he heard the simpering voice call out, "A shame, sir—a real shame, to hesitate over a trifling matter of a few dollars, when you are so near to solving this baffling mystery."

Grizz paused to breathe in the night air, clearing his head, and then he made a call on his cell phone. "Dorothy? I have something you and the teens will want to look at." Next, he tried to call Dirk, but there was no answer. Grizz churned over the engine in his old van and started up the road toward the Surfside Hotel.

Detective Kwan was waiting in the lobby, seated next to Wire, who was again accompanied by his laptop. Maeve came down from her room and joined them a minute later.

"Where's Jessa?" Ms. Kwan asked.

"She didn't tell you?"

The older woman cocked an eyebrow.

"She went to see the Long Beach fireworks."

"Took a cab?"

"Uh, not exactly."

"So someone drove her. . . ?"

"Yeah, guess so." The black-clad girl was obviously being evasive.

"Someone named Dirk?"

The girl nodded. "I called and told her about this meeting . . . they're on the way back here."

"She should have informed me before leaving." Ms. Kwan was clearly not amused. "I may have had a bout of illness but I am still the official chaperone for this trip."

"I know, and she's normally so responsible. I thought for sure you knew." Grizz didn't trust the girl's innocent voice—and he definitely didn't trust his protégé.

While they waited for Dirk and Jessa, Grizz explained to the three others about his encounter in the restaurant with the photographer and the significance of the photo that showed Joe Nui surfing—with his leash on the wrong ankle.

"That is a good clue." Dorothy Kwan's smile warmed his heart, making him forget his annoyance with Dirk. "It makes it pretty obvious that he didn't just die in a surfing accident. Someone else attached the leash—after he was already dead. And we can surmise a bit more about the perpetrator: he or she didn't know a lot about surfing. You should be a private eye, Grizz."

The heavy glass door of the lobby flew open and Jessa strode into the room, a curious expression on her face. A few moments later, Dirk skulked after her. He had his hood drawn up, but Grizz noticed the boy's left eye was swollen.

"What happened?" he whispered to the younger man.

"Misunderstanding," Dirk mumbled. "Rather not talk about it."

Grizz wondered if the shiner would be gone by the time Keisha got back. He grinned; if not, Dirk would have some explaining to do.

Grizz quickly explained to Dirk and Jessa what they'd been talking about and then handed the picture of Joe Nui and Guido to Ms. Kwan. "Know who this guy is?"

She nodded. "Wire, can you pull up a file on Mr. Zarducci?"

A moment later, the man's face appeared on the screen, in the three-view format of a mug shot. Wire whistled. "This guy has quite the record."

Dorothy Kwan glanced at the screen and explained, "Seems he has a long career doing 'collection work' for the mob."

"Do you mean, 'mob' as in 'an offer you can't refuse'?" Maeve asked.

"Mob like, 'sleeps with the fishes'?" Jessa added.

"See what I have to put up with?" Dorothy looked at Grizz. "Five months with this club—we can never, ever have a straightforward discussion."

"What's that in Guido's hand?" Jessa was looking more closely at the photograph.

"Money," replied Wire.

"Who's handing money to who?" Maeve wanted to know.

"*Whom*," Ms. Kwan corrected, as she pulled a magnifier out of her purse and squinted. "Can't be sure, but I think Guido is giving it to Nui."

"He borrowed money from the mob?" Dirk looked impressed.

"Maybe." The detective turned to the CSC members. "As of tonight, you kids are off this case."

"But there is no case," Maeve retorted. "So how can we be 'off' a case we were never 'on'?"

Ms. Kwan shook her head. "It looks like the Mafia is involved. You've already gotten mixed up with too much danger and violence on your previous cases. So we're going to get back into vacation mode and leave this mystery to the authorities."

"Who will do nothing, because someone has scared them off—or paid them off," Grizz noted, sadly. He observed how the CSC members quickly made eye contact with one another, and he grinned, remembering his own teen years. *These kids may have plans of their own.*

Back in his room, Wire tried again to contact QT-AnimeChick. No luck.

A knock sounded on the door. "Come in."

Jessa and Maeve slipped into the room. "Wire—you've gotta help us."

"With what?"

"Solving this mystery, silly."

"But you just heard Detective Kwan—"

"You know she said that just to avoid liability for the PD. Besides, you're the legendary Wire, the guy who hacked into the Pentagon on your PDA."

"School gossip. Never happened."

"You tellin' me straight up you never did anything that was—ah—unconventional?" Maeve challenged.

"I'm busy."

"You don't look it."

"I'm trying to get hold of QT."

"Any luck?" Jessa asked, more softly.

He shook his head.

"Remember back in school, when I told you I saw her picture in a teen model magazine?" Jessa asked, still gently.

He nodded.

"What I was trying to tell you is . . . well, I don't think that's really her picture she sent you. I think . . . the person who calls herself QT sent you an image scanned from a magazine."

Wire was silent a moment. "But I don't care what she looks like," he said finally. "It's okay if she's fat or ugly or—whatever. I just like *her*. She's totally smart and funny and caring."

It was the girls' turn to be quiet. Then Maeve ventured, "Sometimes people on the Internet aren't who they say they are."

"Think I don't know that?"

"Have you considered that QT might not exist? Maybe someone is just trying to get into your head . . . or your system."

For a moment, Wire was afraid he might cry. The girls shifted their feet uncomfortably. Then Jessa suggested, "I don't think you're going to meet with QT on this trip. But we can still do something valuable with our last few days here. We can solve the case—see justice done for this murdered surfer."

Wire sighed. "What do you want me to do?"

"Some more digging into the files on Guido Zarducci," Maeve replied. "Find out where this guy hangs out. I'm sure you can find stuff like that by getting into the police files."

Wire remained motionless.

"Please, Wire?" Jessa asked, in her sweetest voice.

"Why don't you get your buddy Dirk to help you? He's so cute and brave and all."

Jessa frowned. "You're our *real* friend."

"Well. . ." Wire reached for the laptop next to him, flipped open the case. "Let's see if this hotel's lousy excuse for WiFi will let me connect."

Apparently, it did. A few minutes later, Wire said, "Looks like Guido hangs out mostly at two places: a restaurant called Michelangelo's and a pool hall called Sharky's."

"Great," Maeve gloated. "Can you drive us there?"

"When?"

"Now."

"No way. It's late, I'm tired, and Ms. Kwan said—"

"Don't tell me you've lost your sense of adventure?" Jessa interrupted.

"If I do this, you both owe me."

"Totally," Jessa agreed.

"Anything," Maeve added.

Shaking his head, Wire asked, "Michelangelo's or Sharky's?"

"Sharky's—sounds more interesting," Maeve replied.

He closed the laptop, pulled his PDA off the stand, and quickly searched for a map and guidance program. "You better keep this where I can see it," Wire said, handing the PDA to Maeve.

"You got it, boss."

"Don't call me that—especially tonight. And we're just hanging out. Don't do anything to get us in trouble."

"You know us." Jessa looked insulted.

"That's right, I do. And that's why I'm worried."

Forty minutes later, the rented van pulled up alongside a seedy looking street in North Hollywood. In front of them, a blinking red neon sign said Sharky's.

"Think we're gonna get carded?" Wire asked.

"Just make it clear that you're with us," Jessa replied.

"How come you're gonna get in?"

The girls didn't reply; they were already headed for the door, and there was no bouncer at the entrance to challenge them. Inside, cigar smoke hung heavy in the air, giving the dimly lit establishment a foggy, surreal atmosphere. *They still allow smoking in this place—yuck.* Every few moments, Wire heard a *clack!* as pool balls knocked into one another.

He glanced around and saw several men huddled near the bar. "There's Guido," he said quietly to the girls.

"You two shoot pool. I'll get acquainted with Mr. Mafia," Maeve whispered.

Jessa and Wire glanced at each other nervously. Jessa shrugged. "Pick a table."

"You any good at this?" Wire asked.

"I can sink the balls pretty good. Yourself?"

"Only played the electronic version. How do I hold this stick?"

"Oh dear."

The two played pool—or rather, Jessa played pool, wiping the balls off the felt-covered surface so quickly that Wire rarely got a shot. They both kept glancing toward the bar, where Maeve, wearing a back-baring blouse, quickly gained the attention of the scary-looking older man.

"Oh-oh—is this good or bad?" Jessa wondered, as the three men from the bar, accompanied by Maeve, headed toward their pool table.

"You with her?" Guido Zarducci sounded like a robot. His eyes were utterly expressionless, a lit cigar glued to his lips. He pointed his left hand at Maeve.

"Yeah," Jessa's apparent calm masked whatever else she was feeling.

"Too bad."

Wire's heart skipped a beat. *Looks like Maeve blew our cover—and it only took a couple of minutes.*

The man's right hand disappeared into a pocket. Wire saw the outline of something angular, pointy

. . . aimed directly at Jessa. The other two men also had their hands in their pockets. Wire was pretty sure they weren't playing with their change.

"Step into the alley with me . . . real quiet." Zarducci's whisper was ghostlike. "Make any commotion, and . . ." He didn't need to finish the sentence.

Wire could see tomorrow's LA Times headline: Three Arizona Teens Found Dead in Hollywood Alley. *We're toast.* His knees knocked, and he struggled to control his bladder. *At least try to die with dignity*, he told himself.

"Hey Guido," a handsome, younger man spoke up, "no need to trouble yourself. I'll take care of this."

Zarducci hesitated.

"I'll take 'em round the corner and make sure they disappear . . . real good."

"Okay, thanks, Joey."

The shorter man glared at the three young people. The gun concealed in his suit was almost touching Maeve's back. "Now, you three do just what I tell you or I put a slug through one of these bats. You don't wanna see Goth girl's insides splatter across the room, do you?"

They shook their heads.

"Out the back way, real slow. Don't get ahead of me.'"

They did as he asked.

A few moments later, they had walked out the back of the pool hall, down an alleyway, and around a corner, all in the sort of silence Wire had never experienced anywhere but a nightmare. His mind raced desperately. *Can I reach the PDA on my belt . . . send an IM to Ms. Kwan?* But he dared not for fear the man would see him and pull the trigger. He didn't want Maeve's death on his conscience—not in a million years. Better to wait, take what comes.

Then the man turned to them and said, "Holy mother of God, what are you three nut-cases doing?"

"Huh?"

"Who do you think you are, talking to a guy like Zarducci? You would have gotten yourselves killed if I hadn't been there."

Maeve tried to explain, "We're with the Crime Scene Club . . . from Flagstaff, Arizona, we're . . . uh—"

" You kiddies are playin' detective?" the man interrupted. "You do know how close you just came to gettin' offed?"

"Too close," Jessa agreed.

"What were you tryin' to do in there, anyway?"

"Investigate a murder." Wire didn't think he'd ever heard Maeve's voice shake like that before.

"Who's the vic?"

"A surfer, named Joe Nui."

"What's the time of death?"

"Day before yesterday, around one in the morning."

The man shook his head. "These guys aren't the perps."

"You're certain?" Jessa asked.

"What kinda question is that? Course I'm certain. I was with 'em. They was high-rollin' in Vegas that night."

*Well, that eliminates one set of suspects: Guido Zarducci and his Mafia pals have alibis.*

"Gimme that phone." The man pointed to the cell on Maeve's belt. "I wanna talk to your mom or dad."

"Uh . . . Mom's in Arizona. Probably drunk. She probably won't much care what I'm doing."

"You kids have an adult watching you?"

"That would be Detective Kwan, Flag PD."

"Well, get her on the phone. Now!"

Maeve, unusually compliant, pressed a speed dial button and handed her phone to the man. "Hello, Detective Kwan? Joey Russo, LAPD. I'm working shadow on the mob, and I've got three teens here, claim they're in some kinda detective club. They pretty near got killed tonight . . . and they coulda blown my cover." A pause. "All right, I'll release them to you, but I don't *ever* wanna see their faces within a hundred miles of here. You got that?"

He handed the phone back to Maeve. "Maybe you kids can play cop'n'robber in Podunk where ya come from, but this ain't the sticks—understand? Those are real bad guys, and they'd as soon smoke ya as look at ya. So get outta LA—*now*—while you're still in one piece."

Driving back to the hotel, Wire reflected on his changing priorities for the trip: first he had hoped to meet QT. Then he had thought they might solve a crime. And now he just hoped to get home alive.

# Chapter 6
# CAN'T GET MUCH WORSE

Grizz couldn't help but notice the chilly atmosphere at the table where he sat with Dirk, Dorothy Kwan, and three unusually quiet teens. Apparently they had gotten into some serious trouble late last night.

They were gathered for lunch at Bob's Seafood Safari. An enormous stuffed specimen of a great white shark floated on chains suspended from the ceiling, its beady eyes staring at the crowded tables below.

"Well," Dorothy said in a subdued tone, "we know that Guido Zarducci wasn't the killer."

"Wish I hadn't wasted money on that picture," Grizz muttered.

"Elimination of suspects is part of solving crimes," she tried to comfort him. "Even dead-end trails need to be explored."

"Any new leads?"

"Miss Kwan?" Wire spoke up tentatively.

"Yes?"

"I hope you don't mind—especially after last night, but—"

"You have something new?"

"A closer look at our initial evidence."

"Go on."

The boy pulled his laptop out of a padded case, set it on the table, and flipped it open. "I was bored this morning, so I downloaded some new software," Wire explained. "One is an enhancement program that modifies 8 pixel images to 12, and then I added synoptic automontage software, to superimpose images shot on a curved surface and create composite pictures incorporating the diverse planes into a single—"

"Explain that in English, Brainiac," Dirk interrupted. His shiner was even more obvious today.

"I can get closer, better images with the pictures I took at the crime scene," Wire explained. "Like this."

The monitor on Wire's laptop revealed an odd pattern, like tire tracks in flesh.

"What are we looking at?"

"The outside of the vic's right leg, just below his wetsuit. These markings only go for an inch and a-half, on one side."

"How big are these marks?"

"Small enough we failed to notice them, very shallow. They'd hardly show up, unless you view the images with enhancement technology. I ran a program that accentuates depths and contours on a surface."

"Looks like he was lying on a piece of rope," Grizz suggested.

"On the beach?" Jessa asked.

"Nope. Nothing like that at the site," Wire answered.

"The strappy thing attached to his board?" Maeve asked.

"Leash," Dirk corrected. "No way. It's smooth plastic."

"So," Detective Kwan thought aloud, "it would seem the body lay on a piece of rope for some time before its final ride on the waves. Where would you likely have cordage like that lying around?"

"On a boat," both Grizz and Dirk replied at once.

"There's more." Wire touched a key, changing the image on the laptop screen.

"Ooh!" Jessa slid back from the table. "You've ruined this meal—totally."

The monitor showed the wound on Joe Nui's forehead, magnified so big it looked like a red and pink canyon.

"What are these?" Ms. Kwan pointed a finger at several greenish-gold colored specks.

"Metal flakes of some sort," Wire answered. "That's what I wanted to show you. We didn't see these when observing the body, nor in the life-size shots, but with the images enhanced and superimposed onto a single plane. . ."

"What kind of metal is that?" asked Grizz.

"Brass?" Detective Kwan ventured.

"Or copper?" Grizz suggested.

"Could be. Hard to tell. They're awfully small. Still, " Ms. Kwan turned to Wire, smiling, "this is an excellent clue. Whatever killed this unfortunate man, the object left traces. I don't think it was a piece of rock."

"And it isn't a piece of surfboard," Grizz added.

"My appetite is ruined. Can we please put that away?" Jessa's face was white.

Wire shut the notebook case. "I have to go to the can. Excuse me."

Grizz looked across the table at Dorothy. "So—where's our case now?" he asked.

"We can form a hypothesis, thanks to the evidence in these enhanced photos," she answered him. "Joe Nui was hit—hard—by some sort of semi-sharp object, made of brass or copper. Then, some-one laid his body in the bottom of a boat, took it for a ride, and dumped the corpse overboard to drift into the beach. The perp wanted it to look like a surfing accident, but didn't know a lot about the sport—so he or she failed to wax the board, and attached the leash on the wrong foot."

"How come the Neptune coroner didn't come up with all this?" asked Grizz.

"I can't believe the coroner's report missed so much evidence," Ms. Kwan replied. "I hate to say it, but I'm convinced someone in Neptune is covering up a murder. Now the vital question is—covering up for whom?"

"Think it was the Loco Motion gang?" Jessa asked.

"Hard to say," Dirk replied.

"Terrapin said Joe owed them," Grizz pointed out. "They had a motive."

"How about that guy who came into your shop—Terrapin?" Maeve asked. "You said Joe owed him four grand—that's a lot. Think he could've done it?"

"Nah." Grizz shook his head. "He's my bro."

"But," the black-haired girl protested, "the first rule in this game is—trust no one."

Grizz tried to defend his old friend. "Why would he identify Joe's picture? That doesn't make sense."

"To throw you off?" Jessa suggested.

"What about Brandee?" Ms. Kwan asked.

"Too many dead brain cells," Maeve answered. "That woman's head is fried."

"Unless her lush act is a put-on?" the detective wondered.

"Both Brandee and Terrapin suggested that Joe owed lots of people," Jessa said. "How many others might have motive?"

"Could be all sorts of folks," Grizz agreed.

"Doesn't make the case any easier." Dorothy sighed.

"Especially with only two days left to crack it," Jessa added.

The waiter delivered their plates. They stared at the steaming seafood, glanced at the closed computer. No one felt particularly hungry anymore.

After a few reluctant stabs at her crab cake, Jessa suddenly asked, "Where's Wire? He's been gone awful long for a pit stop."

They stared at one another.

"Excuse me, sir." Detective Kwan caught the attention of a waiter as he hurried by, "Have you seen the young man who was sitting with us?"

"Looks kind of like John Lennon?"

"Yes."

"He left a few minutes ago, with four other guys."

"What?"

"They were hanging out by the back of the restaurant, all dressed in black and white, baggy clothes, hair nets. They didn't exactly seem his style."

"Oh, no!" Jessa exclaimed.

Detective Kwan flipped her cell open. "I'm calling to report an abduction."

*Oh great,* Wire thought. *I didn't ever want to see these goons again.*

He was sandwiched between two enormous guys, each at least twice his bulk. They stared ahead like statues. The driver, shaved pate covered with a black bandanna, focused on the road ahead of him. As the pimped-out Charger crawled through the streets, the stereo emitted a deep thump-thump beat that echoed Wire's heart.

The gang member in the front passenger's seat, apparently their leader, turned around. "So, the Neptune cops, they's all over us 'cause that body on the beach. And I ask myself, 'Why is that?' What you think?"

Wire had to take several gulps of air before hesitantly replying, "I don't . . . know. . . ."

"*¡Guero!*"

Wire felt something sharp on his Adam's apple. Without moving his head, he glanced down at a gleaming knife blade, held by the guy on his right. *Okay, if there's Anyone out there, don't let this car hit*

*any bumps. . . .*

"Better tell me straight up, or my homey might just slip."

"We. . ." Wire licked his dry lips, tried again. "We know that Joe Nui owed you money."

The man in the front glanced at the one holding the knife toward Wire's throat. "He don't talk enough, Cuz. Better use that fila and loosen his tongue."

"Oh no, no," Wire said in a rush. "I can talk lots more. Uh . . . we did tell the Neptune PD something about what we heard, but . . . uh . . . we didn't want to, ah . . . inconvenience you guys or . . . anything . . . like . . . bad. . ." Wire's voice faded away.

"So ya really think we iced that surfer in the cove?" The guy sounded matter-of-fact.

*What does he want me to say?* "Oh, no. I don't think so . . . just . . . we have to consider all the possibilities, you know? Not that . . . you guys are like . . . a real possibility, I mean . . . oh, man." Wire gulped; he couldn't manage to get out any more words.

"Know what, little boy?" the leader asked. "This is your lucky day."

"It is?" Wire's voice was a squeak.

"Yeah. Normally, a snitch like you, we'd off ya like that." He snapped his fingers, and Wire felt the knife press slightly harder into his throat. "But we in a peacin' mood, right, Homes?"

The man next to Wire nodded, not releasing the knife.

"We in such a good mood, we gonna let you go, dog."

"Ah. . ." Wire gulped. "That's good. Thanks."

"In fact, we gonna do more than that. We gonna pointcha in the right direction."

"Phat!" the gang member on Wire's left affirmed.

"So listen good while I skool ya," the leader continued. "Tell the pigs we ain't done nothin' to Joe Nui. Yeah, he owed us. But he was all right, he was one righteous vato." He paused for a minute, took out a cigarette, and lit it. "I miss Joe. You wanna know who smoked him?" He took a few more puffs, apparently waiting for an answer.

"I . . . ah . . . yeah, of course," Wire stammered.

"No one saw who did it, but word on the street is, that rich actor who's been seein' Brandee. He mighta offed him." The leader took another drag. "Thassa good tip, ain't it?"

"Boo-ya," the driver agreed.

"Worth somethin', dontcha think?"

The one with the knife nodded.

Wire felt a tug at his belt; then the guy on his right handed Wire's PDA to the leader. "This enough to say thank you, Jefe?"

The leader nodded. "Sweet."

Before Wire realized what was happening, the back left door flew open and strong arms hurled him onto the pavement.

Groaning, he crawled to the sidewalk, struggling to catch his breath.

*I've been beat up by these monsters, held at gun point . . . and now my PDA's gone. I spent weeks programming that thing, had all my favorite games on it, almost as good as a laptop. And it's gone—just like that. What could possibly be worse than this?*

# Chapter 7
# THE TIGER'S TAIL

Back at the hotel, Grizz gazed sympathetically at the bruised young man. He may not be an athlete, but Wire's been through more than most folks his age—and that's just in the past three days.

Maeve held an ice-pack on Wire's bruised shoulder, and Jessa gently massaged the base of his neck, both girls oozing sympathy. Dirk sat on the couch across from them, glaring at the skinny, bespectacled boy. Dorothy Kwan sat on a chair beside Wire, deep in thought.

"Tell me again what the Loco Motion gang said about Nui's death?"

" Ouch. Take it easy, Jessa." Wire turned toward the detective. "They said some rich actor having an affair with Brandee Zam might have killed him."

"Think we should trust these guys?" Dirk asked, contemptuously. "They're workin' awful hard to get the cops off their tail."

Grizz agreed. "Hard to know if we should believe them."

"A wealthy actor, having an affair with Brandee..." Jessa looked thoughtful. "Who would that be?"

"I'd say lots of actors are wealthy," Maeve pointed out, "and actors are a dime-a-dozen in this part of the world."

"Any rumors in the gossip rags?" asked Detective Kwan.

Jessa shook her head. "Shamed to admit it, but I do look at those. Brandee's been out of the news for a while now."

A thought flashed in Grizz's mind. "Peter Lonnie!"

"Huh?"

"That sniveling paparazzi offered to sell me some real pricey photos—wanted an even grand—claimed they were the key to this whole thing."

"You have a way to get in touch with him?" Detective Kwan asked.

Grizz felt a business card still in his pocket. "Yeah, but I don't have that kinda dough."

"You think Mr. Lonnie's pictures might point us to this possible perpetrator?"

"I've got a feeling."

"All right," the detective said. "I have a credit card for Crime Scene Club, and I think I can justify a thousand dollars—for a good cause. Call Lonnie."

An hour later, Peter Lonnie was walking out the glass door of the hotel lobby, grinning like the Cheshire cat as he ran his left hand through a stack of bills in his right. Grizz glared after him.

"Open the envelope—let's see the picture," Maeve begged.

Grizz carefully parted the clips holding the top of the large manila envelope and pulled out a big, glossy image.

"Ooh!" Jessa exclaimed.

"Pretty hot stuff," Maeve agreed.

"Looks like a scandal if I ever saw one," Wire said, wincing as he moved to get a better view.

"Who's the man?" Dorothy Kwan asked.

"You don't know?" Dirk was incredulous.

"Lance Grant," Grizz said.

"I've heard of him, but—"

"Former film star, multi-millionaire, and now running for the national Congress," Grizz filled her in.

Maeve whistled.

"Well, the Locos were telling the truth about one thing—he obviously knows Brandee Zam," Dorothy said, "but is there any reason to think he might be the killer?"

"He had motive," Wire replied. "If Grant's running for Congress, and Joe Nui threatened to expose an affair with his wife. . ."

"Yes," Jessa agreed. "He had reason to silence Nui. Makes me think of our last case." She looked unhappy, as though the memory was painful.

"Remember what Brandee said about a sudden upturn in her fortunes?" Maeve added. "If this guy's a multi-millionaire—"

"She's getting more than romance," Dirk agreed.

Grizz stroked his chin. "I'm going out on a limb here, but the murder itself seems like something this guy might cook up."

"How's that?"

"Well, he's an actor. That means he's good at faking reality. He's been in enough cheesy surf films to put this stunt together. He got Joe's wetsuit and new board—from Brandee, no doubt—dressed the corpse and leashed the board to Joe's ankle. But he's not a real surfer, so he didn't think to wax up the board or put the leash on the left foot."

"It makes sense that Brandee's in on it," Jessa agreed. "Her sudden good fortune could be hush money. She probably forged that note about going surfing, and—voila!—the perfect cover-up for a murder."

"Also explains the Neptune PD," Grizz added. "Lance Grant has a ton of clout, in addition to his fortune. He's in the perfect position to buy off the coroner and chief of police in a small town—get them to rubber-stamp Nui's death."

"We have a decent theory," Dorothy Kwan agreed, "but nothing like a case, yet."

"So what do we do?" Grizz asked.

"I think I'll call both Brandee Zam's and Lance Grant's agents, tell them we'd like to speak to Brandee and Lance, together, about Joe Nui's death," the detective replied. "There's still no official case, and there may never be one, if the authorities are in this man's pocket. But if I request a meeting, I think they'll be very curious to hear what we say."

"Hey, wait a minute." Wire winced again as he stood. "That's fine, but I want to have *some* fun on this trip. Our time in California is almost over. It seems like I've been unofficially declared the CSC punching bag—beat up, threatened at gun point, dumped out of a car, and my PDA stolen. How about we make one little trip for Wire, before you do this thing with Lance and Brandee?"

Dorothy nodded sympathetically. "What do you want to do?"

"Trip to the Spy Store, in Beverly Hills."

"You've got it. You three go this afternoon. Meantime, I'll put in some calls and set this meeting up." She flipped open her phone.

"Dorothy?" Grizz put his hand gently on her wrist. "I've heard a lot about Lance Grant—and you've seen the power he has over authorities. I hear he's one bad dude when someone gets in his way. I'm worried about what could happen to you and the kids if you cross him."

The detective looked unhappy. "I know. But how do I walk away now? I can't let the guy get away with murder, can I?"

Wire spent several glorious hours purchasing miniature electronic devices. He tried to explain to the girls what these technological wonders were and what they were good for, but the two didn't pay much attention. Maeve wandered over to a nearby store with black leather and studded jewelry in the window, and Jessa kept looking for movie stars walking down the sidewalk.

When they returned from Wire's shopping trip, Ms. Kwan told the teens that Brandee and Lance were both willing to meet with them. Early in the evening, the CSC drove through the big electronic gates leading to Lance Grant's La Jolla mansion. It was bigger and more tasteful than Brandee's residence.

As they pulled up, Wire glanced out toward the sea, behind the mansion. "Check out the big boat."

A long, low yacht floated in the water next to a pier.

"How far are we from Neptune Cove?" Jessa wondered.

"About ten miles," Ms. Kwan replied.

"If Joe Nui died here, it would be easy for Lance Grant to take the body onto that boat, cruise up the coast, and dump it where it would float into the cove," Wire reflected.

"I wish we had a warrant—I'd like to compare the rope markings on the victim's body with evidence in that yacht," Ms. Kwan agreed.

A servant waited for them outside the door, then welcomed them and led the four down a set of long hallways, into a spacious room with a big picture window looking to the sea. The walls were covered with posters from Lance Grant's movies. The couches and chairs' bright colors and crisp lines looked modern and European. A large marble coffee table in the center of the room held several books and a sculpture.

Brandee Zam and Lance Grant each stood by separate chairs. Mr. Grant was dressed in a sweater and slacks, looking as poised as if this were a photo shoot. He smiled a movie-star grin and gave each member in turn a firm handshake. *A real politician,* Wire thought.

Brandee looked considerably better than she had at the time of their previous visit, wearing a retro-style dress with her hair well coifed and makeup tastefully applied. "Nice to see you again," she said.

"Please be seated," Mr. Grant added. "I understand you wish to talk with us about the tragic fate of Ms. Zam's late husband. I know you met with her before and had some concerns about the actual cause of his death. But I'm not sure how this concerns me?"

"You might understand better after you see this." Ms. Kwan handed Lance Grant a copy of the picture they had purchased from Lonnie.

Lance looked at the picture, not a trace of expression on his face, and then he passed it to Brandee, who gasped.

"Where did you get this piece of filth?" the movie star asked.

Ms. Kwan told him.

Lance Grant shook his head. "You're a detective Ms. Kwan, I'm sure you appreciate how easily digital images can be manipulated. Because you aren't from here, you probably don't realize that many of the pictures these unethical characters sell are fakes. No doubt someone—I might guess Peter Lonnie—has taken advantage of your naiveté. He's been trying to sell false pictures of me to the magazines for some time now." His voice became quieter, edged with steel. "I've informed *The Enquirer* and others that printing doctored images, like this one, would result in their financial ruin."

"Then you deny any romantic relationship between yourself and Brandee?"

"We have been friends for several years. It's common for celebrities in the film and music industries to be well acquainted with one another. She called me after your visit, upset that Joe's death might be a murder. I told her that I wanted to be a friend and support her. But nothing unethical or inappropriate has happened between us. We are friends— nothing more or less. It's a shame the American public has no esteem for affection, preferring titillating—though unreal—images like this." He pointed to the picture with a look of disgust on his handsome face.

"Did you know Joe Nui?" the detective asked.

"Everyone knew Joe. Unfortunately, he abused Brandee's good graces, and he came to me—and others—asking for money. However, I pick my charitable giving rather carefully."

"So he was angry with you?"

"I do not wish to be disrespectful," he said, looking at Brandee.

Brandee shrugged. "Joe had problems—with lots of people. Lance and Joe were casually acquainted. But—what's this meeting really about? I don't recall anyone from the police saying there is a criminal case, and we aren't suspected of anything—are we?"

Ms. Kwan didn't answer her directly. "An analysis of photographic evidence, taken at the cove, suggests Joe was killed by means of a semi-sharp metal object, then dressed in his wetsuit, laid in a boat, and dumped off the coast—giving the superficial appearance of an accidental death."

"Is this an official police report—or just the result of your overactive imagination, Detective Kwan?" Lance Grant was no longer smiling. "By the way, I believe your jurisdiction is out of state, is it not?"

Ms. Kwan was unruffled. "We're just trying to help by lending our expertise."

Wire's attention drifted to the center of the room. He squinted, trying to get a better focus on what he was seeing.

"Are you helping us—or falsely accusing us?" Grant frowned. "I realized long ago that unscrupulous people—from all walks of life—will produce fake documents, crackpot theories, and terrible lies, in order to discredit those richer and more successful than themselves. I see that you are one of those types—and you have overstayed your welcome."

Wire jumped up. "Excuse me!"

Everyone turned startled faces toward Wire. He crossed the room and ran his fingers over a cast metal sculpture of a dolphin, leaping from its base on the coffee table. "Lovely sculpture you have here."

Grant's frown deepened. "Why, yes, it is called *Liquid Grace.* It's by the famous artist, Roger Grayland."

"Mmm. Nicely polished. Bronze?"

"Yes, but I don't understand how any of this relates to—"

"There are tiny metal flakes in the wound on Joe Nui's head," Wire explained. "And this sculpture is carefully polished—except here." He ran a finger over the top of the dolphin's fin. "This dorsal fin is exactly the size of the object that smashed into the victim's skull and—odd coincidence—the statue is jagged just at this point. It's missing a few tiny pieces. Can you explain that, Mr. Grant?"

Grant folded his arms. "Sad to say, a servant dropped that sculpture while cleaning it. A shame, but most guests don't notice. You have quite the sharp eye, son—to go along with your active imagination."

Maeve leaned forward. "Can we talk to the servant?"

"No. You cannot talk to the servant, nor can you intrude any further in my home. I invited you people here trusting your good intentions. I'm sorry to see I was wrong. You come in with some sort of insane theory that I'm a murderer. You're upsetting poor Brandee in her time of grief."

"Mr. Grant—" Detective Kwan began, but he cut her off.

"Look, lady, kids—you're messing with the wrong man. I've spent decades defending myself against falsehoods, and I'll do it again now. When I have time, in a day or two, I shall call my lawyers. I am accusing you all of harassment, libel, slander, and whatever else they advise." He turned a cold gaze toward Ms. Kwan. "Detective, I suggest you begin searching for a new career—I don't think anyone else will hire you as a policewoman after they learn of this fiasco. You can also say good-bye to this silly little club of yours. No one will dare touch it with a thirty-foot pole after I'm done suing." He pushed a button on the wall, and two tall men built like refrigerators in suits appeared in the doorway. "Gentlemen, get these troublemakers off my property."

A few minutes later, they were back in the van driving out of the mansion gates.

"Way to go, Wire," Maeve accused. "Couldn't you have kept that discovery to yourself?"

"They're both getting away with murder," Jessa lamented.

"Do you think he meant what he said about suing?" Maeve wanted to know.

Ms. Kwan looked grim. "I'm afraid he did."

"Does he have a case?" Wire asked.

The policewoman nodded. "I'm out of my jurisdiction. I have no authority to be investigating this case—and I certainly have no authority to involve you kids."

Wire shifted uncomfortable in his seat. "I'm terribly sorry, Ms. Kwan, I shouldn't have—"

"It's my own fault," she interrupted. "I should never have gotten involved in this—and never have involved all of you. I fear this was my worst—and my last—example of professional misjudgment."

"But it's so wrong," Jessa said, suddenly angry. "The police are covering up an innocent man's death, and all we've tried to do is get at the truth."

"Welcome to the real world," Maeve said wearily, as though she spoke with the experience of decades, "where 'truth' is whatever the rich and powerful say it is."

"Isn't there anything we can do?" Jessa protested.

Ms. Kwan shook her head. "We stepped on the tiger's tail—and I'm afraid he's about to devour us."

# Chapter 8
# DOWN TO THE WIRE

Grizz stopped by the hotel the following afternoon, to catch up on the case. He found three despondent teens and one devastated adult. After hearing their troubles, he told them, "You can't always win, but you can always surf."

Maeve rolled her eyes. "That's a lot of help."

"No, I mean it. The ocean has a way of restoring beaten souls. Sun'll be up for a while. Who wants to try it?"

Jessa's face lightened. "Promise no dead bodies on the beach?"

"Maybe jellyfish."

"I'm up," Jessa agreed.

"Me too," Maeve assented.

"I'll pass," Dorothy Kwan said, and Wire did likewise.

"Hey, wait a minute," Jessa added. "I don't see Dirk. Is he surfing too?"

Grizz chuckled. "Dirk is . . . let's say, he's preoccupied. Keisha got back into town this morning, and some of her friends apparently told her something about Dirk pursuing an out-of-town girl,

so . . . Keisha and Dirk are having a long, serious conversation." He chuckled again. "It'll just be you two newbies and old Grizz in the water this afternoon."

Hours later, the three bobbed up and down on foam beginners' boards in the gentle ocean swells. Jessa and Maeve had paddled out to meet a wave, jumped up, and fallen too many times to count. But they came up laughing and persisted at trying again. Now, they could each stay up for brief intervals—and they were beginning to experience the thrill of surfing.

Grizz noted the deep swooshing sound before the others; long years of experience told him to squint into the horizon. "Gnarly wave coming, girls. Might want to duck under."

"Whoa—that is a big one!" Jessa exclaimed.

*She's sounding like a surfer*, Grizz thought. *Have they really forgotten all the trouble they're in?* He hoped so.

"Hey ocean—come and get me!" Maeve shouted, bouncing up and down on her board.

A wall of thundering liquid rose up and raced toward them. They turned shoreward and paddled furiously. Grizz saw the wave overtake Jessa. She angled her board just right, caught the motion of it, and jumped to her feet, balancing unsteadily but quickly enough to stay atop the tiny flying vessel. Maeve, next in the lineup, screamed and laughed, held onto the rails with all her strength, and leapt nimbly atop the hurtling stick. The next instant, Grizz deftly maneuvered into the curl and, using a minimum of energy, flew toward the beach, salt spray caressing his cheek. For a glorious moment, the two new surfers and the old master flew together, in formation, harnessing the vast rolling force beneath them.

*This is what life is all about—this is what makes it worthwhile.*

Then Maeve toppled, still screaming gleefully, into the water, and Jessa lost her balance a moment later. Grizz smoothly rolled off his board so he could make sure the other two came up all right.

Jessa popped up first, still grinning. "This is awesome, Grizz!"

Maeve surfaced sputtering.

"You all right?" Grizz asked.

"Cool ride," she gasped back. "But I took a big gulp of salty ocean."

"It's been great—but I think I need to rest," Jessa added.

"A wise surfer knows when to come in from the water," Grizz told her. "We'll call it a day—and a great start for you two mermaids."

As they loaded the van, Jessa glanced at her cell phone. "Text message from Ms. Kwan." She read it aloud: "Return to the hotel immediately. Something's come up."

Wire watched out the hotel lobby window as the old van pulled up, and Grizz and the girls climbed out. *The geek's gonna get some respect on this trip, after all,* he told himself.

As soon as they entered the room, Ms. Kwan asked Grizz and the girls, "Have you seen the news?" Their blank faces said no, so she nodded to Wire. "Got that video clip ready to play?"

He turned the screen of his laptop toward the others and tapped at the pad. A CNN reporter announced, "Startling news today as Brandee Zam, the pop singer, reported to the La Jolla police department the alleged murder of her husband, Joe Nui, at the hands of movie star and congressional candidate Lance Grant."

The reporter turned to the woman standing beside him. "Jill, you've been covering this from La Jolla all day. What can you tell us?"

"Well, Ted, several hours ago Ms. Zam burst into the police department. She told officers that Lance Grant murdered her husband, striking him with a statue. She claims that he forced her to dress her husband in a wetsuit, tie him to a surfboard, and the two of them set the body adrift to look like an accident."

"Did she explain her reason for coming forward with this story?"

"It appears Brandee wanted to make a deal—immunity from prosecution in exchange for her testimony."

"If I recall, the death of Brandee's husband was regarded by the Neptune PD—where the body was found—as an accident."

"That's right, Ted. Sources in Neptune say the coroner there has been giving red-faced explanations as to why they didn't report foul play in Joe Nui's death."

"Jill, do we have any word from Lance Grant on this affair?"

"Mr. Grant's office has offered no comment at this time."

"And there's another twist to this story involving a paparazzi?"

"This is an exclusive break, right here on our station, Joe. This man—step toward the camera, sir—is a photographer. What did you say your name was?"

Peter Lonnie stepped into the forefront of the scene, his eyes bulging, smiling like he'd died and gone to heaven.

Wire turned off the video transmission. "I've seen it three times—sick of watching this part."

"Why do you think Brandee confessed?" Jessa wondered.

"I've been wondering the same thing," Detective Kwan replied. "I think Wire knows more than he's telling me—but he wouldn't say anything until we were all here."

"You know something about this?" Maeve asked him.

"There is another video that I, ah, just happened to stumble across," Wire said, slyly. He touched the pad again.

A grainy image filled the screen: Brandee and Lance, dressed as they had been for the previous day's meeting. They stood facing each other in the ocean-view living room where the CSC had confronted the pair.

Brandee screamed in a shrill voice, "You promised, you said 'everything's spotless.' You told me, 'I'll handle it.'"

"Calm down," Lance shot back.

"How come that lady and those kids know so much?"

"They don't 'know,' they're just guessing. Besides, the very threat of legal action scared them off."

"They know about this." She grabbed the dolphin statue with trembling hands. "They have pieces of the fin stuck in Joe's head. Why didn't you just shoot him for God's sake?"

He yanked the bronze sculpture away from her. "Settle down. They'll never get a warrant—I paid the Neptune PD a lot of dough and no one's going to crack. Besides, I'll make this statue disappear."

Brandee was growing more hysterical. "I should never have listened to you. I'm still young—still beautiful—I have a career ahead of me. If the cops come again, they'll take me to jail." She dropped into a chair, sobbing.

"Oh, shut up." The actor was clearly unaffected by her hysterics. "Your career is deader than Elvis—deader than Joe is, too."

"Murderer!" the singer shrieked.

"With your help, you conniving she-devil. We're both in this together, and don't you forget that."

The video ended. Ms. Kwan, Grizz, and the girls looked from the now-black screen to Wire's face.

"Has Brandee seen that?" Jessa wanted to know.

"Well," Wire said, a twinkle in his eye, "everything I'm telling you now is just my guess—you understand. I would guess that *someone* sent a copy of this to Brandee Zam in an e-mail, along with the suggestion that she quit trusting Lance Grant to keep her safe and instead surrender to the tender mercies of the authorities."

Detective Kwan asked, very quietly, "How did *someone* get that video in the first place?"

Maeve gasped, "At the Spy Store, you bought that—"

"I bought lots of stuff," Wire cut-in.

"You bought that little camera and transmitter thing, about the size of a pen."

Wire shrugged.

Ms. Kwan had an icy tone in her voice. "I don't suppose you still have that?"

"Gee, Ms. Kwan, I seem to have lost it."

"Strange, isn't it?" She was clearly not amused.

"Very odd," Wire agreed.

"I wonder if you left fingerprints on it when you 'lost' it?" the detective asked.

Wire smiled. "I don't think there were any prints on it."

The detective shook her head. "I would never, under any circumstance, advocate an illegal surveillance."

"*Whoever* did this, you knew nothing about it," Maeve smirked.

"But if that video wasn't legally obtained, there's no evidence against them," Jessa pointed out.

"You know that, because you're an intelligent young woman who cares about the law," Grizz remarked. "Brandee didn't look very rational on that tape—and it sounds like she wasn't very rational when she ran into the police station."

"I don't suppose *someone* did anything else with that tape?" Ms. Kwan asked, wearily.

"Well, I would guess—just a theory, you know— that *someone* might post it anonymously on the

Internet. Not knowing the source, it won't serve as evidence, of course, but it could definitely influence opinions."

"What do you think will happen with the Neptune PD?" Grizz asked.

"There's bound to be an investigation," Ms. Kwan answered him. "And the case will transfer to La Jolla where the crime apparently took place."

"Do you really think they'll convict him?" Maeve asked. "All the evidence is circumstantial. He probably got rid of that statue already. He's got a ton of dough—I see him getting off."

"We have to be realists," Wire agreed. "There've been some famous cases where celebrities walked free despite a bucket of blood linking them to a crime. However, the public isn't easily fooled. Lance Grant's reputation will never be the same again, whether he serves time or not. And I can assure you he won't be hassling any of us—he's got plenty of his own problems now."

"I guess," Jessa ventured, "the moral of the story is: Be careful who you choose to be your partner in crime. Lance Grant was cool as ice, but Brandee flipped under pressure."

"I would say the moral is: What goes around comes around," Grizz ventured. He smiled, and then turned to Ms. Kwan. "You have one last night here, and the case seems to be wrapped up. I don't suppose, Dorothy, that you would care to accompany me to a private dinner? I think these young people can fend for themselves this evening."

She smiled. "I'd love to, Grizz. You have a place in mind?"

"I know a very roma—reasonable—little restaurant in San Pedro."

Jessa and Maeve giggled.

As soon as Grizz and Ms. Kwan had left, Jessa said, "Who'd have guessed?"

"Wonder where that will lead." Maeve turned to Wire, who was closing his laptop. "So Wire—you got any ideas what we should all do tonight?"

He didn't answer.

"Wire?"

He was staring out the window. Jessa and Maeve followed his gaze and saw a pretty girl, in a miniskirt and high-heeled patent leather boots, reaching for the hotel lobby door.

"Excuse me," the stranger said as she came in. "Is Wire here?"

He stood as in slow motion. "QT?" His voice was a whisper.

"Yeeah!" She grinned. "You look just like your picture. And by the way, now that we're in real space, you can call me by my name—it's Meeka."

"Meeka," Wire repeated. "You can call me . . . Wire."

"I'm so sorry we didn't get together earlier. It's been the worst week you can possibly imagine. I took my laptop to ComicCon, and somebody stole it! Then—this is so awful—I dropped my PDA in a toilet and it shorted. I thought I was gonna totally die—it's been like living in the twentieth century for four awful days."

"Horrible," Wire agreed.

"So anyway," QT-Meeka gushed on, "I purchased a new mini-mother board at an electronics shop,

but that wouldn't interface with standard carriers, so I had to reroute the settings to the old random access matrixes those cheap servers use. By the time I received your messages I was embarrassed and I wanted to totally surprise you—so I hacked into the locator code for your laptop and used GPS to find you here." She flashed another grin.

"You do . . . stuff . . . like that?" Maeve was flabbergasted.

"Oh, hi! You must be Wire's friends. So thrilled to meet you." She smiled at Maeve and Jessa.

"I hope this won't seem rude, but—did I see you once in *Teen Beauty Magazine*?" Jessa asked.

"Yeah, I did a couple fashion modeling gigs. But I quit doing that because if people think you're a model, they don't respect you for your intellect—you know? For some reason people still think if a woman is beautiful, she doesn't have it up here." She tapped her forehead.

"People are so lame," Wire agreed.

"So." Meeka grabbed the boy's arm. "Can I show you the town?"

"You bet."

"You ladies want to come?"

Jessa and Maeve declined.

"By the way," Meeka asked, heading out the door, "have you been following the news about Brandee Zam and that murder? Who would ever have guessed?"

Maeve and Jessa exchanged looks and shook their heads. "You got that right," Maeve said. "Who would have ever guessed?"

FORENSIC NOTES

CRIME SCENE CLUB, CASE #5

# CHAPTER 1

## Evidence List

## Vocab Words

| | |
|---|---|
| animated | patron |
| ascending | itinerary |
| emancipated | inane |

## Deciphering the Evidence

While Wire drives, Maeve carries on an *animated*—or spirited and lively—conversation with Jessa, who is sitting behind them.

The flock of tattooed bats *ascending* from Maeve's waist appear to be rising up and flying out over her shoulders.

Wire tells Maeve she should go to court and get *emancipated*, like he did. He has been granted certain legal rights of adulthood—in this case, the right to live without the supervision of parents or guardians—even though he is not yet an adult by the standards of the law.

Members of the Crime Scene Club have the chance to go on a vacation thanks to the club's wealthy *patron*. A patron is a person who uses money to help someone or something, such as an institution an event, or a cause.

Wire is tired of having to go along with the girls' list of places to visit; he argues that it is his turn to pick the *itinerary*.

In Wire's opinion, surfing is pointless; he's not about to drown himself for this *inane* macho sport.

## The World of Forensics

Our English word "forensic" comes from the Latin word *forensis*, which means "forum"—the public area where in the days of ancient Rome a person charged with a crime presented his case. Both the person accused of the crime and the accuser would give speeches presenting their sides of the story. The person with the best forensic skills usually won the case.

1.1 Forensics technicians utilize a variety of scientific techniques to gather evidence, such as this dusting method to detect latent fingerprints. Forensic evidence is commonly used in court proceedings as a type of reliable "witness."

In the modern world, "forensics" has come to mean the various procedures, many of them scientific in nature, used to answer questions of interest to the legal system—usually, to solve a crime. Detective Kwan and the members of the CSC have used many of these procedures in their cases. Although Wire doesn't know it yet, in this case, their fifth, the procedures involved with forensic photography will prove to be particularly useful to them.

## Forensic Photography

Using photographs to document evidence is important for many types of cases. The photographs can be used to simply record the surrounding conditions and evidence at the time of the crime—but they can also be taken back to the lab, where computers are used to enhance details on the photographs that might not otherwise be discernable to the human eye.

Recent advances in digital imaging have greatly improved many aspects of forensic photography. Digital techniques allow detectives and the lab technicians who help them to capture, edit, output, and transfer images faster than they could with processed film. In the old days, when photographers depended on darkrooms, many techniques had to be applied through time-consuming trial and error; now, with digital photography, these techniques can be instantly applied on a computer, and the results are immediately visible on the monitor.

# CHAPTER 2

## Evidence List

## Vocab Words

disposition
idiosyncrasies
pro circuit
legendary
karma
skeg
objective
perp
protégé
stoic

## Deciphering the Evidence

Grizz is used to Dirk's sour *disposition*; he knows the teen's usual mood is a rather gloomy one.

Although Dirk has some quirky traits, Grizz is able to overlook his *idiosyncrasies* and appreciate his finer qualities.

Grizz won't give Dirk a cigarette because he knows that smoking is prohibited on the *pro circuit*. Pro circuit is short for professional circuit, a series of professional competitions in different locations.

When Dirk refers to Grizz as the *legendary* soul surfer, he is implying that Grizz is extremely well-known for his surfing ability.

**111**

Grizz senses good *karma* when he meets Wire. In this instance, karma refers to a feeling or an aura, based on something about Wire's life experiences and his actions.

Dirk wonders if the deep gash on the dead man's temple was caused by his *skeg*. The skeg is the fin on the rear bottom of a surfboard that is used for steering and balance.

Wire explains to Grizz that if they can stay *objective*, not letting their personal feelings get in the way of the facts found at the scene, they will have a better chance of finding out what happened.

Maeve tells Dirk that the scars on her legs and chest are from the time a *perp* sabotaged her brother's sports car, which she then drove off a cliff. Perp is short for perpetrator, or the person who commits a crime.

Dirk became Grizz's *protégé* when Grizz took him off the street and helped him find his way in society. A protégé is someone whose welfare and training is promoted by an influential person.

The female officer tried to show appreciation for Wire's picture-taking, but the male officer remained *stoic*, showing no emotion when Wire offered to burn the photos onto a flash drive for them.

## What Does a Coroner Do?

A coroner is a public official who investigates and determines the cause of death, especially in cases when the death is not due to natural causes.

## Forensic Procedures Used in CSC #5

### Preserving the Crime Scene

The first police officers at a crime scene usually have the task of preserving or securing the scene. If the crime scene is not properly preserved, evidence could be lost or contaminated. The officers seal off the area around the body by closing doors or putting up yellow police tape. Only investigators involved in collecting evidence will be allowed inside this perimeter.

Once the site is secured, the responding officers wait for the investigative team to arrive. While waiting, the officers record notes about the crimes scene—especially about anything that might be different once the crime scene investigators arrive. Finally, these first responders are also responsible for recording the time of notification, observing any bystanders, and identifying and separating witnesses.

# Documenting the Crime Scene

Forensic photography is one of the most important first steps in documenting any crime scene. In doing this, every photographer must make quick decisions about the correct lenses, lighting, and viewpoints in order to collect the most accurate total image of the scene. The best shot of the scene might include a combination of a panoramic shot from the center of the scene, aerial shots, and images taken from a witness's point-of view. Wire begins by photographing the overall scene, including the cove from every direction. He then moves closer to the body and again shoots from many different angles. Finally, he gets close-up shots of the gash on the forehead.

While Wire is photographing, Maeve records notes and GPS coordinates that describe and place each image. Both CSC members know that if the images are needed as evidence later, they will need careful documentation.

# Gathering Evidence

Once the overall images are completed, the crime scene investigation can move inward toward the victim. The crime scene has to be thoroughly searched for evidence that might provide a clue about the cause of death or about the identity of victim or suspect. Even the most insignificant piece of garbage may hold a significant piece of DNA.

Any evidence that is found has to be handled carefully so as to maintain the chain of custody.

The chain of custody of evidence is the record of all people who have come into contact with that evidence. In a criminal case, the fewer people who handle the evidence the better, but if evidence must be handled there are particular protocols that must be followed to preserve any trace evidence, fingerprints, or DNA evidence that may be present. In maintaining the chain of custody it is also vital to keep a clear written record of exactly where and when individuals did come into contact with the evidence.

## More About Forensic Photography

### Establishing Scale

Forensic photographers need to get the best images of the whole scene and then be able to switch focus down to clear images of tiny latent fingerprints or fiber particles. Wire and Maeve add a ruler to the full scene image, to add scale information to the shot. Because the ruler's length is known, it provides a point of size comparison and may also help later to prove the image is authentic and unaltered. In addition to size scales, photographers add gray scales, color grids, and compasses into images to set or compare color and indicate direction.

Scale is also important for images of objects that are very small. When an image is focused in on a tiny object, the eye has no reference point to indicate size. Therefore, an object of known size, such as a quarter, is often added to a close shot to show scale.

## Global Positioning Satellite Receiver

The Global Positioning System (GPS) was developed by the U.S. Department of Defense, using a constellation of satellites circling the Earth to transmit precise microwave signals to GPS receivers that allow users to determine exact locations, time, speed, and distances. When this information is combined with digital photography, the location coordinates (longitude and latitude) can be embedded on the photographs like a date stamp. This means the location can be exactly placed on a map.

## Quick Reminder

The lines of longitude and latitude allow human beings to know exactly where they are on the planet. Longitude lines run north to south (but measure east and west), starting at 0° at the Prime Meridian in Greenwich, England, and progressing to 180° eastward and −180° westward. Lines of latitude run east to west (and measure north and south), starting at 0° at the Equator and going to 180° at the Earth's poles.

# CHAPTER 3

## Evidence List

### Vocab Words

haggard
rudimentary
lateral
subtle

## Deciphering the Evidence

When Detective Kwan meets the teens in the lobby to discuss the morning's adventure, she appears *haggard*. Even though she is dressed professionally as usual, her illness makes her look worn out and tired.

Dirk observes that the dead man's surfboard is free of wax, prompting Wire to think to himself that Dirk might have a *rudimentary*—or primitive—brain after all.

The board used by the mystery man lacked *lateral* strength. Because it was weak on the sides, it would have been damaged from hitting the man on the head hard enough to cause his fatal injury.

Dirk tells the Crime Scene Club teens that when Loco Motion, the group of thugs at the beach, decides to hurt someone, they're not very *subtle* about it. Subtle means hardly noticeable; the injuries they would cause would be very noticeable.

## Forensic Science Used in CSC #5

## Autopsy

An *autopsy* is a postmortem medical examination that is performed on a body to determine the cause of death (COD) as well as the circumstances surrounding death. A coroner, medical examiner, or forensic pathologist will perform a medical legal, or forensic, autopsy in cases when a death is suspicious.

The first step in the autopsy is to determine the body's height and weight. This information gets recorded along with age, sex, race, and hair and eye color. All of this information can help identify an unknown victim like the surfer. Next, the medical examiner performs an external examination of the body, looking for evidence of trauma. Other marks on the body, such as tattoos, scars, or birthmarks that might identify the individual, are also recorded. Also at this time, the medical examiner removes hair samples from the body and collects any trace evidence found on the body. After the external examination is complete, the coroner more closely examines any trauma to determine the cause of the injury.

Once all injuries have been measured, photographed, and documented, the examiner begins dissecting the body. This is traditionally done with a Y-shaped incision down the front of the chest. All internal organs are removed, weighed, and examined. Blood is collected for typing, DNA analysis, and toxicology testing. Other bodily fluids may also be collected for toxicology testing. Stomach contents may be removed for testing to help determine the time since death. Finally the head and brain are examined. Once all organs have been thoroughly checked, they are placed back inside the body and the incisions are sutured shut.

After the examination is completed, the coroner must file an official autopsy report, which summarizes her findings. The report will include details on the examination, all photographs that were taken during the autopsy and any conclusions that have been drawn about the cause of death. This report is a legal document that might be used if the case is ever brought to court.

## More About Forensic Photography

Crime scene photographers have to document the scene exactly as it is so that images can be used as evidence, which is important for many types of cases. The

## Why Do Police Call Nameless Victims "John Doe"?

When identities of victims are not known, it is helpful for law enforcement personnel to have a name they can use when speaking or writing about the individuals in the case. It is believed that the use of the name "John Doe" for victims whose identity is not known originated in England in the 1300s. A legal document from this period calls a hypothetical (not real) landowner "John Doe." An unknown female is referred to as Jane Doe, and an unknown baby may be called Baby Doe.

photographs can be used to simply record the surrounding conditions and evidence at the time of the crime—but they can also be taken back to the lab, where computers are used to enhance details on the photographs that might not otherwise be discernable to the human eye. Detective Kwan and Grizz are going to alter Wire's images of the surfer's face to try and help identify the victim.

# CHAPTER 4

## Evidence List

### Vocab Words

choreography
jurisdiction
demise
expertise
palatial
faux
concoction

## Deciphering the Evidence

When Wire puts down Brandee Zam, Jessa scolds him, saying Brandee has a fine voice and some clever *choreography* in her videos. Choreography is the art of creating and arranging dances.

The Neptune Police Department has not yet interviewed Brandee Zam about her husband's death, because she lives in La Jolla, which is outside their *jurisdiction*. Jurisdiction is the geographical area over which a court or governmental body, such as a police department, has authority.

The Neptune PD promises Detective Kwan that they will talk to the Loco Motion gang about Mr. Nui's *demise*, or death.

Detective Kwan convinces Brandee Zam that she and the members of the Crime Scene Club may be able to use their *expertise* to help her learn more about her husband's death. They have the *particular* skills and knowledge to investigate a crime scene, even if they will be doing it unofficially.

Brandee Zam lived in a *palatial* mass of stone and glass. Palatial is related to the word *palace*, and suggests a dwelling that is as fancy and as spacious as a palace.

Brandee's mansion was surrounded by *faux*, or fake, Greek statues, meaning they were made with something other than marble.

Her servant gave Brandee a glass filled with a mixture of different ingredients, and she quickly drank the *concoction*.

## Forensic Procedures Used in CSC#5

### Interviewing

When she begins speaking to Ms. Zam, Detective Kwan uses a tone that is businesslike but sympathetic. She knows the first rule of interviewing is to establish rapport, or a feeling of mutual trust. Since the main purpose of a witness interview is to obtain information that is relevant and useful to the case, Detective Kwan proceeds to question Ms. Zam to see what she can find out. When

4.1 At one time in the United States, police interrogators were allowed to use coercive tactics, such as bright lights, food deprivation, or abuse to get a suspect to confess. However, in 1966 the Supreme Court reaffirmed legislation against abusive or coercive police interrogations with the case of Miranda v. Arizona.

the woman says her husband's death was an accident, Detective Kwan doesn't take what she says at face value, asking, "What makes you so sure it was an accident?" Even when Ms. Zam rambles on about how much Joe loved surfing, the detective keeps the focus on trying to get information that would be helpful to the investigation.

Ms. Zam's drinking made her a difficult witness to talk to. Investigators must be prepared to deal with witnesses who may not offer much information, who may be lying, or who may be emotionally distraught and unable to clearly remember or communicate what they know about the matter in question or the people involved. Some witnesses will be more helpful than others, but just as every lead should be followed, even if it turns out to be a dead end, every witness is potentially a source of information that could make all the difference in a case.

# CHAPTER 5

## Evidence List

Vocab Words

vagaries
notorious
compromising
paparazzi
incomprehensible
evasive
surmise
liability
compliant

## Deciphering the Evidence

Grizz is puzzled by the *vagaries* of the opposite sex; he has trouble keeping up with the unpredictable behavior of women.

Peter Lonnie, the photographer who pulls up a chair next to Grizz at Trader Tom's Tiki Paradise, was *notorious* up and down the California coast. Notorious means well known, but usually in an unfavorable way.

For the right amount of cash, Lonnie wouldn't hesitate to expose his own mother to shame or disgrace by selling *compromising* pictures of her.

Peter Lonnie was a member of the *paparazzi*. Paparazzi refers to freelance photographers who specialize in taking pictures of celebrities, particularly ones that show their private lives. The term *paparazzi* comes from the name of a fictional photographer, Signore Paparazzo, in the Italian film La Dolce Vita.

Lonnie tries to tempt Grizz into buying the third photograph by saying it is the missing piece of the puzzle that will make the *incomprehensible* obvious. Comprehend means understand, so incomprehensible means difficult or impossible to understand.

When Detective Kwan questions Maeve about Jessa's whereabouts, Maeve is *evasive* in her response. She is trying to avoid giving a direct answer.

The photo showing Joe Nui surfing with his leash on the other ankle leads Detective Kwan to *surmise* that the perpetrator didn't know much about surfing. To surmise is to guess or speculate about something.

Maeve tells Wire that Detective Kwan ordered them to go back into vacation mode to avoid *liability* for the police department. Detective Kwan knows that the police would have legal responsibility for any dangerous or harmful incidents involving the teens.

Maeve is unusually *compliant* when the man from Sharky's instructs her to get Detective Kwan on the phone. Her fear makes her willing to cooperate with the stranger.

## Where Did the Term "Private Eye" Originate?

The first private detective agency in the United States was the Pinkertons. The company's logo was an open eye surrounded by the motto, "We Never Sleep!"—which inspired the term "private eye."

## Forensic Procedures Used in CSC

5.1 In 2007, the North Carolina attorney General dropped the charges against three Duke University Lacrosse players who were accused of rape. Alibi evidence, which included time stamped photographs, cell phone records and even ATM receipts were instrumental in the case.

**Case #5**

## Using Alibis to Eliminate Suspects

A person who is suspected of committing a crime may offer an alibi—an excuse that he or she was somewhere else when the crime took place. For an alibi to be convincing, the person's statement should be supported by other people, who can vouch for the suspect's whereabouts, or by other evidence (such as phone records or restaurant receipts) that indicate where the suspect was when the crime was committed.

# CHAPTER 6

## What Is the History of the Mafia?

The Mafia is a society of organized crime that is believed to have its roots in the mid-1800s in Sicily, Italy. When the European feudal system collapsed in Sicily in the nineteenth century, there was no real governing authority, and so landowners and other powerful men began to emerge as leaders. They used the threat of violence to enforce their authority over farmers, and thus began the Sicilian Mafia. When Italians emigrated to the United States during the late nineteenth century, a branch of the Mafia developed on America's east coast.

## Evidence List

Vocab Words

tentatively
hypothesis

## Deciphering the Evidence

Wire speaks up *tentatively* at lunch the day after the incident at Sharky's. He has some new information, but brings it up hesitantly because he's not sure how Detective Kwan will react.

The evidence in the enhanced photos allows Detective Kwan to form a *hypothesis*, or possible explanation or theory for what happened to the dead surfer.

## Forensic Procedures Used in CSC Case #5

Forensic Photography

Enhancement has always been a part of photography. Traditional methods of image enhancement include contrast and brightness adjustment, burning and dodging, cropping, and color balance adjustment. Computers and modern technology allow for some additional means of image enhancement.
Enhanced images give excellent infor-

mation, but will not necessarily hold up in court. A forensic photographer will usually be required to testify that the image is an accurate and unaltered representation of the crime scene. Any alterations to the image call its validity into question. Because Wire's enhanced images probably will not hold up as evidence, the team needs additional, hard evidence to prove the death was no accident and to catch the suspect.

## Trace Evidence

A thorough search for trace evidence is vital to any crime scene investigation. Seemingly insignificant things—tiny threads, hairs, dust, pollen, flakes of metal and glass—can make all the difference when it comes to solving a crime.

The coroner should have collected trace evidence such as hair, blood, or metal flakes from the body during the autopsy. However, nothing about any metal flakes was discussed in the official report. The team is only able to see them because of Wire's image enhancement software, which reveals the tiny flakes in the forehead gash. Detective Kwan is surprised that the coroner could have missed these flakes as well as the rope marks on Joe Nui's leg. The coroner would have had equipment sophisticated enough to analyze the metal, and thus could have provided an essential clue about what type of object might have caused the wound.

# CHAPTER 7

## Evidence List

### Vocab Words

incredulous
clout
unethical
naiveté
titillating
superficial
unscrupulous
harassment

## Deciphering the Evidence

When Detective Kwan doesn't recognize the man in the third photo, Dirk is *incredulous*, finding it hard to believe that she doesn't realize the man is former film star Lance Grant.

7.1 The potential for digital manipulation poses challenges for forensic photographers. Forensic photographers must adhere to strict guidelines in order to preserve the integrity of an enhanced image if they are to submit it for court evidence.

Grizz tells Detective Kwan and the teens that Lance Grant has a ton of *clout*. He has the power and influence to buy off the coroner and chief of police in the small town of Neptune.

Grant refers to the paparazzi as *unethical* characters, suggesting to Detective Kwan that he wouldn't put it past them to do something dishonest or immoral such as sell photos that have been manipulated.

Grant is implying that Detective Kwan is inexperienced or unsophisticated when he says that someone has taken advantage of her *naiveté*.

Grant says that the American public likes *titillating*—or exciting—images such as the one Grizz bought from Peter Lonnie, even if what it portrays is not real.

According to Detective Kwan, an analysis of photographic evidence suggests that whoever killed Joe Nui was trying to give the *superficial* appearance of accidental death. The perpetrator wanted it to look—at least on the surface—like it was an accident.

Grant accuses Detective Kwan of being immoral, comparing her to the *unscrupulous* people who produce fake documents, crackpot theories, and terrible lies to discredit those who are richer and more successful than themselves.

**131**

Grant tells Detective Kwan and the teenagers that he will call his lawyers and accuse them of *harassment* for causing emotional distress to him and Brandee Zam for no legitimate reason.

## Forensic Procedures Used in CSC #5

### Establishing Motive

Determining who has a motive—a reason—to commit a crime helps detectives identify suspects. Motive alone is not proof, but when combined with "means" (the ability) and the "opportunity" to commit a crime, it can lead to a jury conviction.

### Obtaining a Warrant

In the United States (as well as in many other countries, including Canada and the United Kingdom), certain citizen rights are legally protected. In the United States, these rights are guaranteed by the Constitution and the Bill of Rights. A warrant, however, allows police to cross these legal lines.

A warrant is an authorization written by an officer of the court (usually a judge), which commands an otherwise illegal act that would violate individual rights; it grants the person who carries out the warrant protection from any legal damages. The most common warrants are search warrants (which give the police permission to search someone's private property when there is reason to believe that evidence connected to a crime will be found there), arrest warrants (when police bring a suspect into custody until a court officer determines what happens next), and execution warrants (when a convicted person receives a death sentence).

A typical arrest warrant in the United States would be worded something like this:

> This Court orders the Sheriff or Constable to find the named person, wherever he or she may be found, and deliver said person to the custody of the Court.

7.2 If incriminating DNA evidence is found at a crime scene, but there are no name matches found in the criminal databases, a "John Doe" arrest warrant identifies a perpetrator according to his genetic code. This allows prosecutors to file charges against an unnamed suspect.

# CHAPTER 8

## Evidence List

Vocab Words

preoccupied
conniving
advocate
rational
anonymously
circumstantial
realist
matrix

## Deciphering the Evidence

When Jessa asks about Dirk, Grizz tells her
that he is *preoccupied*. Dirk is distracted by
other concerns.

On the video secretly taken by Wire, Lance
Grant can be seen calling Brandee Zam a
*conniving* she-devil. He is accusing her of
being no less devious and scheming than he
is.

Detective Kwan tells Wire that she would
never *advocate* an illegal surveillance. It
would go against acceptable legal procedure
to support or defend such an activity.

Grizz remarks that Brandee didn't look
very *rational* on the tape. She was behaving

in a manner that suggested she was not capable of reasonable or logical thinking.

Wire tells Detective Kwan that someone may have posted the videotape *anonymously* on the Internet, meaning they did it without identifying who was posting it.

Maeve wonders if Lance Grant will be convicted, because the evidence of the case is *circumstantial*. Circumstantial evidence is evidence having to do with the circumstances surrounding an incident, as opposed to the facts as observed by eyewitnesses.

## What's the Difference Between Libel and Slander?

Libel and slander both involve the concept of defamation, which is communication that harms a person's reputation in an unfair way. Libel generally refers to more permanent communication, such as writing, print, signs, pictures, films, CDs, DVDs, and blogging. Slander refers to more fleeting communication, such as a spoken statement. However, if the statement is broadcast over the radio or TV, it is usually considered libel rather than slander because the message can reach an audience as large as or larger than a message in a printed publication.

Wire and Maeve think Lance Grant will go free because of his celebrity and wealth, saying, "We have to be *realists*." A realist is someone who accepts the way things are and deals with it accordingly.

Wire's new friend QT/Meeka speaks in the same techno-geek language that he does, talking about such things as random access *matrixes*. In the world of computers, a matrix is a type of virtual grid containing rows and columns of information. A multiplication table can be thought of as a kind of matrix.

## What Is Immunity from Prosecution—and How Does Someone Get It?

When someone who is involved in a crime agrees to provide testimony or evidence in exchange for not being prosecuted for any criminal act he or she may have committed, that person is said to have been granted immunity from prosecution. Sometimes it is worth letting a witness go unpunished if that witness's testimony can help solve a big case. For example, a drug dealer's testimony could help bring down an entire illegal drug operation, which would be more beneficial to society than prosecuting a single drug dealer.

## When Is Surveillance Legal—and When Isn't It?

Laws governing electronic surveillance are different from state to state. Most states allow the recording of telephone calls and other electronic communications as long as at least one person involved is aware and has okayed the recording. At least sixteen states require "two-party" or "all-party" consent. It is illegal in all fifty states to record a conversation you are not part of, have not received permission to record, and could not naturally overhear. At least twenty-one states outlaw the use of hidden cameras or video recorders in private places.

Law enforcement officials are given more leeway when it comes to surveillance. They are permitted by law to obtain a court order to tap into a telephone if there is enough reason to believe that criminal activity is being conducted.

## Wrapping Up CSC Case #5

In this case, the teens of Crime Scene Club learn that things are not always what they seem in life. The man on the beach appeared at first sight to be the victim of a surfing accident. But the teens' forensic training has taught them to never make any assumptions, and always look beneath the surface. Grizz and Dirk provided valuable clues based on their expertise in surfing, and Wire used his skills in forensic photography to capture important details before the crime scene was washed away by the tide.

The Neptune Police Department and Coroner were also not what they seemed. Instead of being the trusted officials a community depends on in a time of tragedy, they were more than likely involved in a cover-up. It appears that they were being paid to keep quiet by a wealthy celebrity and aspiring politician, who—beneath the powerful and glamorous image he projected—was actually a murderer having an affair with a married woman.

Wire's Internet friend, QT, is the final example of things not being what they seem. QT may have been a former Teen Beauty Magazine (ital) model, but Jessa and Maeve could tell when she started talking about computers, that she and Wire were on the same wavelength.

With the case closed, Wire finally has some time to enjoy himself with his new friend Meeka before the members of Crime Scene Club head back to Flagstaff to see what's in store for them next.

# FURTHER READING

Baden, Michael and Marion Roach. *Dead Reckoning: The New Science of Catching Killers.* New York: Simon & Schuster, 2001.

Ferllini, Roxana. *Silent Witness. How Forensic Anthropology is Used to Solve the World's Toughest Crimes.* Buffalo, NY: Firefly Books, 2002.

Innes, Brian. *Forensic Science.* Philadelphia, PA: Mason Crest Publishers, 2006.

Newton, Michael and John L. French. *The Encyclopedia of Crime Scene Investigation.* New York: Checkmark Books, 2007.

Robinson, Edward M. and David (Ski) Witzke. *Crime Scene Photography.* Burlington, MA: Academic Press, 2007.

Ubelaker, Douglas and Henry Scammell. Bones: A Forensic Detective's Casebook. New York: Harper Collins, 2000.

Walker, Pam and Elaine Wood. *Crime Scene Investigations: Real-Life Science Labs for Grades 6-12.* San Francisco, CA: Jossey-Bass, 1998.

# FOR MORE INFORMATION

American Academy of Forensic Sciences. www.
aafs.org

"Becoming a Crime Scene Investigator." www.
crime-scene-investigator.net/becomeone.html

Crime Library, "Trace Evidence" by Katherine
Ramsland
www.crimelibrary.com/criminal_mind/forensics/
trace/1.html

Crime Scene and Evidence Photography
www.crime-scene-investigator.net/csi-photo.html

Cush, Chris D. "Want to become a crime scene
investigator? Here's the real story." www.crime-
scene-investigator.net/RealStory.html

Schiro, George. "Examination and Documentation
of the Crime Scene." www.crime-scene-investiga-
tor.net/evidenc2.html

# BIBLIOGRAPHY

Byrd, Mike. "Crime Scene Photography—Guidelines." *Crime Scene and Evidence Photography*. www.geocities.com/cfpdlab/photos.htm

"Crime Scene and Evidence Photography." www.crime-scene-investigator.net/csi-photo.html.

Genge, N. E. *The Forensic Casebook*. New York: Ballantine Books, 2002.

Groffy, Ronald. "Scale Selection and Placement." *Crime Scene and Evidence Photography*. www.geocities.com/cfpdlab/Scale.htm.

Jaeger, Jens. "Police and Forensic Photography." *Photography Encyclopedia*. www.answers.com/topic/police-and-forensic-photography, 2005.

Lyle, D.P. *Forensics for Dummies*. Indianapolis, IN: Wiley Publishing Inc, 2004.

Owen, David. *Hidden Evidence. Forty True Crimes and How Forensic Science Helped Solved Them*. Buffalo, NY: Firefly Books, 2000.

Wecht, Cyril H. *Crime Scene Investigation*. Pleasantville, NY: The Reader's Digest Association, Inc, 2004.

# INDEX

# PICTURE CREDITS

istockphoto. com
Alms, Brandon: p. 109
Catherine, Nancy: p. 130
Howard, Wayne: p. 133

Jupiter Images: pp. 123, 127

To the best knowledge of the publisher, all images not specifically credited are in the public domain. If any image has been inadvertently uncredited, please notify Harding House Publishing Service, Vestal, New York 13850, so that credit can be given in future printings.

# BIOGRAPHIES
## Author

Kenneth McIntosh is a freelance writer and college instructor who lives in beautiful Flagstaff, Arizona (while CSC is fictional, Flagstaff is definitely real). He has enjoyed crime fiction—from Sherlock Holmes to CSI and Bones—and is thankful for the opportunity to create his own detective stories. Now, if he could only find his car keys . . .

Ken would like to thank the following people:
*Tom Oliver, who invented the title 'Crime Scene Club' on a tram en route to the Getty Museum, and cooked up the best plots while we sat at his Tiki bar . . . Mr. Levin's Creative Writing students at the* Flagstaff Arts and Leadership Academy, *who vetted the books . . . Rob and Jenny Mullen and Victor Viera, my Writer's Group, who shared their lives and invaluable insights . . . My recently deceased father, Dr. A Vern McIntosh, who taught me when I was a child to love written words. This series could not have happened without all of you.*

# Series Consultant

Carla Miller Noziglia is Senior Forensic Advisor, Tanzania, East Africa, for the U.S. Department of Justice, International Criminal Investigative Training Assistant Program. A Fellow of the American Academy of Forensic Sciences her work has earned her many honors and commendations, including Distinguished Fellow from the American Academy of Forensic Sciences (2003) and the Paul L. Kirk Award from the American Academy of Forensic Sciences Criminalistics Section. Ms. Noziglia's publications include *The Real Crime Lab* (coeditor, 2005), *So You Want to be a Forensic Scientist* (coeditor 2003), and contributions to *Drug Facilitated Sexual Assault* (2001), *Convicted by Juries, Exonerated by Science: Case Studies in the Use of DNA* (1996), and the *Journal of Police Science* (1989).

# Illustrator

Casey Sanborn earned his degree in fine arts from the Rhode Island School of Design, in Providence, Rhode Island. Prior to working as an illustrator, he worked for several years at an international publishing company as an Art Director and Illustrator for children's electronic books and multi-media. This is Casey's first foray into illustration for the young adult age group. He currently resides in Chicago, IL where he works from his home studio. To see more of Casey's illustration please visit: www.flickr.com/photos/caseysanborndesign